z

Mud Run

Mud Run

Bill Swan

James Lorimer & Company Ltd., Publishers
Toronto, 2003

© 2003 Bill Swan

James Lorimer & Company Ltd. acknowledges the support of the Ontario Arts Council. We acknowledge the support of the Government of Canada through the Book Publishing Industry Development Program (BPIDP) for our publishing activities. We acknowledge the support of the Canada Council for the Arts for our publishing program. We acknowledge the support of the Government of Ontario through the Ontario Media Development Corporation's Ontario Book Initiative.

Cover illustration: Steve Murray

Canada Cataloguing in Publication Data

Swan, Bill
  Mud Run

(Sports stories ; 60)
ISBN 1-55028-787-7 (bound)   ISBN 1-55028-786-9 (pbk.)

I. Title. II. Series: Sports stories (Toronto, Ont.); 60.

PS8587.W338M83 2003   jC813'.54   C2003-901666-8
PZ7

James Lorimer & Company Ltd.,   Distributed in the United States by:
Publishers   Orca Book Publishers
35 Britain Street   P.O. Box 468
Toronto, Ontario   Custer, WA USA
M5A 1R7   98240-0468
www.lorimer.ca

Printed and bound in Canada.

Contents

*For Mrs. Gilbert and her Grade Five class,
who heard it first.*

And for Kathy.

1

The New School

Matthew Thompson did not like his new school, though he had never set foot in it. He didn't like the way the basketball hoops had been stripped of their netting and the way one bent forward, tipped toward the ground as though ashamed. He didn't like the hopscotch markings painted on the pavement between the portables and the main school building. For that matter, he didn't like the portables either.

Matt had moved to Clarington, on the shores of Lake Ontario, from London (Ontario, not England) during the summer. The move had ruined his vacation, maybe his life. As though he was a pet goldfish, his parents had plopped him into a strange neighbourhood, in a strange house, near a strange school, to start the eighth grade in a school full of strangers. They hadn't even asked.

Ignored at home that Labour Day afternoon, Matt walked to his new school to see how badly he really did hate it. It took four minutes: two to walk four doors down to the park entrance, and two to cross the combined park and playground.

Matt had just turned thirteen. He wore a blue and white Maple Leafs baseball cap to cover a haircut he wished was more stylish. If he wore thick-soled shoes, he was 1.7 metres tall — his grandfather would translate that to 5 feet 7 inches. Matt was slim, with a dimple in his left cheek that he admired at in the bathroom mirror ever since he heard Lillian Fredericks whisper to a class-mate that she thought it was cute. Embarrassing.

Matt was alone in the schoolyard, which was deserted except for a gust of wind that whirled around the corner like a saucy baby tornado, blew sand in his face, and disappeared. Heat from the sun rose from the black asphalt. Matt kicked at small pebbles and listened to the echoes dribbling off the back of the school. Back home in London, he would have been playing two-on-two basketball in Adam Roberts' driveway, or putting together a road hockey team with his friends, or checking out Web sites on the Internet. But his mother had taken over the family computer in her search for new clients, and his friends were far away.

He kicked at a larger rock and watched it roll before it set-tled into the far corner.

"Watch this!" said a voice behind him. He turned to see a boy smaller than himself and with a dirt-stained face. The boy tried to kick an even larger rock as though he were booting a soccer ball. The rock wouldn't co-operate — it was too large — and it rolled lamely and stopped. The boy hopped forward, holding his kicking foot in his hand, his face twisted in pain, his mouth held in a tight straight line to keep sound from escaping.

"I'm watching," Matt said flatly.

"I'm Gavin Richards," the kid said. "You're new. I've never seen you before. You gonna go to school here?"

"Maybe," Matt replied. "I'd rather move back to London."

"I'll bet you can't do a slam dunk," Gavin said, releasing his foot and heading for the basketball nets.

Gavin bounded forward, caught a pole in his right hand and twirled once around, landing on his feet.

"Bet you can't do that!" he yelled with a grin.

"Go home and tell your mother she wants you," Matt said.

Gavin's jeans were ripped at the knee and stained. His T-shirt looked as though it had been worn for several days. He looked exactly like the last day of vacation.

"I'm eight," Gavin said. "But I'm small for my age. I'm going to be in Grade Four this year."

"Go tell somebody who cares," Matt said. He leaped up to tag the bent basketball rim just to show he could. But Gavin had moved on.

"Betcha can't climb up on the portable roof!" Gavin cried. The portables sat in a row, strung together by hydro wires and cables. Matt followed Gavin into the narrow space separating two portables.

"Betcha can't catch this!" Gavin yelled. He stood on the railing around the platform at the back of the portable. As Matt emerged from the shadows, Gavin grabbed the baseball cap from Matt's head and flung it overhead.

Matt watched his favourite hat land on the portable roof. He lunged at Gavin but missed, and the smaller boy bounded away with a laugh. Matt knew he could catch the kid, but why bother?

He turned back. His Uncle Jim had given him that cap for his birthday.

"Betcha can't get up there," Gavin said from the safety of the soccer field. "Betcha can't climb it. Only the high school kids can!"

Matt looked up. He had never climbed a roof before, had never thought of it, knew he shouldn't try.

He stood on the platform and then swung up on the railing. From there he could reach the edge of the roof. With one foot braced against the door frame, he lifted himself high enough to get one elbow over the edge.

Slowly, he pulled himself up. Resting on both elbows, he looked out over the flat, black gravel-and-tar roof. With a lunge he flung himself forward and rolled onto the sun-softened tar.

As if alive, his cap flapped and rolled out of reach. He pulled himself to his feet. Matt noticed he had stained his jeans on one knee. His parents would not be happy. He retrieved his baseball cap. Below him, Gavin strained to see, hopping up and down, still shaking the numb out of his stubbed toe.

"Betcha can't get down!" Gavin shouted, gleefully, and then disappeared. He reappeared on the other side of the portable. Laughing, he ran toward the nearest door and released a rock in an overhand throw.

The rock thudded against the metal door to the main school building, then echoed. Matt watched in horror as the door slowly opened

A thin man in need of a shave held the door open with his right hand and looked left, then right, just in time to see Gavin's heels slip around the corner. Had he looked up, he would have seen Matt, but he didn't.

"I saw you, " the custodian said to Gavin's now-gone heels. "I'll report you." He made no attempt to chase Gavin.

Matt quietly lowered himself flat to the roof and waited.

First he heard nothing: no footsteps, no door closing.

At the sound of wheels clattering, Matt peeked up to see the custodian closing the door of an outdoor storage unit. then turning to push his cleaning cart across the tarmac. Matt ducked, barely daring to breathe. He heard the rattle of keys, and the whole portable shook as the custodian opened the door and entered.

Matt lay on the roof, tar and gravel pressing into his cheek. All he had to do now was wait until the custodian left.

However long that might be.

2

Safe and Home

Matt lay still on the portable roof, waiting. A door closed with a hydraulic *wissssh*, then clicked into place. Below him, empty pails from the custodian's cart rattled. He heard a few shuffling steps; then the jingling of keys as the custodian entered the portable.

Matt dared not breathe.

Below he could hear running water and the slop of the mop on the floor. A strange, tuneless humming. From the roof, he could see the playground in one direction and the tops of the basketball boards in the other. A snarl of wires hung from a wooden pole at the corner of the roof. Why had he done this?

He waited. The cart rattled again, the door clicked shut. Again, keys jingled as the custodian shuffled off to the next portable. Matt decided to take a chance.

Still lying on his stomach, he squirmed backwards toward the edge of the roof. He swung his legs over, resting on both elbows. Slowly, he lowered himself, his toes pointed and legs flailing as he tried to find the narrow railing.

Nothing.

He lowered himself more, knowing that if his feet didn't find that railing, he would have to drop blindly to the platform below.

Lower, lower he went, until he clung to the roof by only his hands. His feet could find no perch. He hung there, arms fully extended. Finally he dropped, taking the weight of the fall on his legs, letting them fold underneath him as he landed.

Immediately he was running, crouching low until he was around the corner of the gymnasium, across the parking lot to the street. If he ever caught Gavin Richards, he thought, he would fix him. Good.

He smiled at the nerve of the kid.

* * *

When Matt arrived home, his mother was in the driveway in her bare feet, washing the van.

"Dad home yet?" he asked, knowing the answer was no. If his dad were home, his parents would be in the kitchen preparing dinner.

"Not yet," she replied, dipping the cloth into the soapy bucket. "Catherine-Marie is studying."

Catherine-Marie, Matt's older sister, was preparing for her last year in high school.

"She's studying the day before school begins?" Matt asked. "Do you think we should get her, like, checked out or something?"

Matt's mother straightened, the back of her hand on her hip. "She's got a hard year ahead of her," she said. "She's trying her best to get started right."

Matt made a snorting sound. "Only my sister would spend the summer reading school books," he said, ducking under the half-open garage door. He blinked. Unpacked boxes filled the shadowy gloom.

"You seen my hockey stick?" He meant, of course, his street hockey stick. Nobody would use a good stick on the road.

"And you talk about Cathy-Marie rushing the season," his

mother laughed. As though she didn't know he played street hockey all year long. With his friends. When he had friends.

She poured the bucket of water on the flower bed, then grabbed the hose to rinse the van.

"It's just in case," Matt said. In case somebody comes knocking on my door. That would have happened back home in London. But not here, in Clarington. It was the kind of name you would give a clown. Clarington the Clown.

"We'll eat when your father gets home," his mother said as she rolled up the hose.

Matt found his hockey sticks bundled with the garden tools in the corner of the garage. "We could have gone to the Exhibition today," he said. "Even with Dad working, couldn't we?"

His mother ran the back of her hand over her forehead. "He's trying so hard to get a start at his new job," she said. "Besides, you and your sister are going to school tomorrow."

"Yeah," snarled Matt. "We need a day of mourning for that."

Matt's mother pretended not to hear.

Matt gave up on his hockey stick and slunk downstairs to the TV room — or what would be the TV room once the piles of boxes were put away. He rifled through one and found some games. An old Rubik's cube caught his attention; he gave it a few twists and tossed it back in the box. Next he grabbed a chess set. He set up the pieces, moved a few, first white, then black. But he found that chess without an opponent had no pulse.

He rummaged through another box, found a deck of cards and began a game of solitaire. He tried the television, but they had no cable yet and there were nothing but snowy images on two channels.

Upstairs, he could hear the sound of his mother in the kitchen stirring up the smells of the evening meal. Matt had completed five games of solitaire and was starting the sixth when his father arrived, hung his jacket in the hall closet and called, "Honey, I'm home!"

By then the smell of dinner — homemade hamburger patties containing onion pieces he knew would be too large — had filled the house for too long. The patties would be like hockey pucks.

"Howdy, Buckaroo," said Mr. Thompson as he started down the stairs to the family room.

Matt's father was a tall man with a thickening waist and thinning mid-brown hair. He wore blue jeans, metal frame glasses, and a faded plaid shirt. He had stopped on the stairs, halfway up, halfway down.

"Dad, 'Buckaroos' went out with Roy Rogers," Matt replied. He wasn't exactly sure who Roy Rogers was, but knew he was a television artifact from before even his father's childhood.

"I'm afraid I have, ah, some bad news," Mr. Thompson said.

Matt stood up, trying to catch his father's eye and failing. "Bad news?"

"I made a few calls," his father said. "You're … um, we're too late to register for hockey this year."

Matt dropped — maybe flopped would be a better word — into the nearest chair.

"Great. That's just great. Now what am I supposed to do all year?"

"It's not as though we didn't try," said Matt's mother from the top of the stairs. "Teams get filled up in June. There isn't enough room for everybody who wants to play."

"Not enough ice pads," said his father. "Or something."

Matt felt a lump rise in his throat.

"Anyway," said Mrs. Thompson, "dinner is ready. Although it is a little overdone."

They ate dinner at the long counter in the kitchen. Catherine-Marie, finally emerging from her room, was the last to sit down.

She was seventeen, with blonde, frizzy hair. Her clothes were rumpled from spending a full day in her room reading.

"What about Cathy-Marie?" Matt asked as the family hunched over their plates.

"What do you mean?"

"Is she going to take her dance and piano lessons?"

"And vocal. Don't forget about vocal," said Cathy-Marie, slurping her soup.

"She gets to do everything," said Matt grumpily. "It's not fair."

"Much of life is not fair," said Mr. Thompson. "But your not getting into hockey has nothing to do with Cathy-Marie's classes."

"Besides," said Mrs. Thompson, "she'll do all that and continue to get straight A's. Won't you dear?"

"I need to if I'm going to go to university next year," she said, absent-mindedly rubbing a crease mark on her cheek.

"You fall asleep with all those books?" Matt asked. "Looks like you've tattooed 'em on your face." He tried to make the remark as a joke, but it came across with an edge, his disappointment over hockey grating like bad chalk on a clean blackboard.

"Children," replied Catherine-Marie, "should be seen and not heard."

"Quit that right now," said Mrs. Thompson. "Stop picking on each other."

Matt answered Cathy-Marie's glare with squinted eyes.

"You studying today?" asked Mr. Thompson, squeezing his hamburger in both hands so the relish ran green and juicy into his fingers. "On Labour Day?"

"*You* worked today," said Catherine-Marie.

"That's, ah, different," replied her father.

"In *your* eyes, Daddy," Catherine-Marie replied. "But studying is work, too, and I want to make sure I'm ready for the start of school tomorrow. Besides, the English class this year is really heavy."

"You have a point. I surrender."

"Anyway, I studied because I wanted to. How come you worked this weekend?"

Mr. Thompson unfolded a napkin and spread it on his lap. "Emergency," he said. "One guy working on this group project didn't show up Friday, then we found he didn't complete what he said he would. And there's supposed to be a big presentation tomorrow with the client. The whole team had to come in for the weekend."

Matt looked up. "You do group work?" he asked. "I hate group work."

"Most projects require several people. It'd be easier to work alone, believe me."

"Group work sucks," said Matt.

Mrs. Thompson offered everyone a second hamburger, which only Mr. Thompson accepted. "Nobody works alone," she said. "Ever."

"You do, Mom," said Matt. "You're down there on your computer all alone …"

"E-mail. I send drafts and notes and pictures back and forth to a dozen people every day on every job. The only reason I still have my clients is because of e-mail." Matt knew his mom's job — writing advertising and promotional copy — meant she needed to use the computer a lot.

"If I had been home," Mr. Thompson asked his daughter "would it have made any difference? Would you still have stud-ied all weekend?"

"Of course," said Catherine-Marie.

Matt exhaled slowly. Surely, he thought, one of them was adopted.

3

Meeting the Teacher

The next day, after a breakfast of cereal and toast, Matt tried to escape his mother's fussings at the door.

"You'll be home at lunch?" he asked her. She nodded.

Matt crossed the street in front of his house and immediately found himself stuck in a small parade. The whole idea of the first day of school angered him.

Matt hated this school, S.T. Lovey Public School. *Back home in London*, he thought, *I'd be shouting across the playground to my friends*.

In the schoolyard, he leaned against a dirty brick wall and sneered. Younger students ran and laughed and jumped and shouted around him. He glowered at them. He watched as friends greeted friends, swapped summer fibs, hollered to others still arriving, all backpacks and lunch bags. Matt knew, he just knew, he didn't belong. He knew no one, he had no friends.

As the first bell sounded, he recognized Gavin Richards in the throng. Matt shook his fist at him, but already the younger boy had turned and disappeared amid other arms and legs in new back-to-school clothes. A teacher blew a whistle and pointed directions, and Matt found himself with twenty-nine other students heading for a classroom.

He shuffled into line and down the hallway. He grimaced as

he took a seat in the back corner by the door, trying to ignore the sidelong curious glances of other students.

Ms. Wellesley, the sign on the door said. His new homeroom teacher was young and quick, with brown hair that bounced when she turned her head, and a smile full of teeth. Matt thought, *I hate happy people*. He grimaced at the smile she flashed at him.

"Good morning, class," she said, limping to the blackboard and printing her name. "My name is Ms. Wellesley, and I'm your teacher for this year."

She paused, her eyes moving around the room, locking gazes with each student for a moment.

"We're going to have a lot of fun this year, but we're also going to work hard." Matt yawned. Teacher talk. She continued, but Matt didn't hear the rest. The first-day-back-to-school morning droned on.

Shortly before morning recess, Ms. Wellesley limped up to Matt's desk.

"How are you making out?" she asked, quietly turning his workbook over so she could see the cover. "You should put your name on here."

"Yeah," Matt replied sullenly.

"I see." She reopened the book, flipped past a couple of blank pages, flipped back to more blank pages, and fixed her eyes on Matt.

"You're not doing too well today, are you?" She hesitated, then added, "Matt."

Matt shifted his eyes to the corner of the room. A girl with a red hair band turned to look at him. He ignored her.

"The math work is in your text," Ms. Wellesley said. "You can always finish that at home. The science notes on the board you should borrow from a friend. You don't want to miss something on the first day."

Matt looked up at his teacher and replied without thinking. "I don't have a friend."

Ms. Wellesley looked at him, this time with no smile. "I'm sure that will be corrected quickly," she said. "Take your time. You can stay as long as you want after school. I'll leave the notes on the board."

"I can get it tomorrow."

She had already begun to move on to the student at the next desk. "Tomorrow the boards will have tomorrow's notes," she said. "If you don't get it all after school, I'll lend you my overheads." She flashed her big-toothed smile. Matt did not smile back.

* * *

Shortly before lunch break, a sharp rapping on the door brought the whole class out of a restless silence. A tall woman with heavy glasses and sensible black shoes stepped into the room.

"I hope I'm not interrupting anything," she said. "I just wanted to visit every classroom this morning to say welcome back and introduce myself to new students." She glanced at Matt and turned to the teacher.

"Ms. Wellesley, it looks as though you have this dynamic Grade Eight class under control. I'm sure you'll all work together to have a wonderful year."

The woman strolled slowly to the front of the room. Matt noted that she looked at every student in the room, one at a time. Matt tried to stare back but failed.

"For those who don't know me, I'm Mrs. MacMillan, and I'm the principal of S.T. Lovey Public School. I hope you all had a relaxing weekend to get rested up for the school year. Let's have a good year."

She paused, and her tone became more serious. "I want you

to remember," she said, her arms folded in front, "that this year you are senior students at this school."

"Wow!" said a boy from the back corner. "You mean we're finally the big guys?" He had orange hair and five rings in his left ear.

Mrs. MacMillan stared down the hubbub that followed. "Ryan Abolins," she said, hands on her hips. She stared until Ryan dropped his eyes. "We should raise our hand to ask a speaker to yield the floor. Even in Grade Eight."

She paused again. "The younger students will look up to you. They will imitate what they see you do. You will be their heroes. That is why it is so important for you to be aware of avoiding inappropriate behaviour. For example, we had a report just this weekend of someone climbing on a portable roof."

"That's the high-school guys," said Ryan.

"What did I say about behaviour, Ryan?" said the principal. "You'll come to my office after school today and we'll discuss it some more."

She returned her attention to the whole class. "I'm sure you already know how dangerous such a climb can be, and that any-one caught could suffer serious consequences. Those who have been here know they can come and see me at any time. New students should know I mean it. If you have any problems that your teacher can't help you with, I'd be happy to see you."

"Blah, blah, blah," Ryan muttered, under his breath.

"And I'll see you at 3:30, Ryan. Be there."

Mrs. MacMillan pulled open the door and stood for a moment with her hand on the handle, her eyes fixed on Ryan like lasers.

"One more thing," she said. "Anyone interested in the run-ning club this year should turn out tonight for a short meeting. We'll introduce your new coach then." She smiled, and Matt saw her exchange glances with Ms. Wellesley.

"Where?" asked the girl with the red hair band from the front of the room. Three times that morning Matt had locked eyes with her; each time, he tried not to blush and was the first to look away.

"Right here, Ashley," said Mrs. MacMillan. "Most of last year's cross-country team is from this class, so I thought that would be easier."

"Where's Mr. Janzen?" asked a boy in a plaid shirt from the middle of the classroom. He was tall and big-boned, wearing a cotton shirt with a pocket over his heart and blue jeans that had been ironed. "Mr. Janzen coached last year."

"What's to coach?" sneered Ryan. "It's running. You just run."

Mrs. MacMillan again stared the class into silence. "Mr. Janzen has been transferred to another school. He isn't here this year, Robert," she said. "But I know some of you were interested in running, so we do have another coach."

"Who?" asked another girl. She had brown eyes and black hair tied back in a ponytail.

"You'll find out tonight, Kathryn," Mrs. MacMillan said. She moved into the hallway, which was beginning to fill with children and then turned to the class one last time.

"Oh, and Matt Thompson, could you come with me to the office? I have some forms for you to take home to be filled out."

As Matt followed her, Gavin Richards ran up the hall toward them. He turned his head to wave weakly to Matt and bumped into the principal.

"Excuse me," Mrs. MacMillan said, reaching out with both hands to hold Gavin by the shoulders and help him regain his balance. "But don't we have a rule about running inside the school?"

"Yes, please, Mrs. MacMillan. But I've got to hurry home for lunch."

"But first we wait until the dismissal bell sounds. And we *always* walk inside the school. Now you go back to your classroom and wait until your teacher dismisses the class for lunch."

Gavin stopped.

"Now."

Gavin grimaced, turned on his heel, and stomped quietly back down the hall.

He was halfway down the hall when the bell sounded, a piercing, shrill, five-alarm bell. Matt watched as Gavin lifted up on his toes, kicked into a sprint, turned the corner, and was gone.

4

The 100-Kilometre Club

By the time the dismissal bell sounded at 3:30 that afternoon, Matt had completed almost all of his science notes. Most students had stuffed books into backpacks and chattered out into the hallway. Four or five remained.

The tall boy with the plaid shirt turned to Matt. "Are you staying for cross-country, too?" he asked. His was the first friendly voice Matt had heard all day.

"Hey Robert," said Ryan. "That new guy's just sucking up to Ms. Wellesley. Besides, we have a good team. Baz will be here tomorrow. We don't need anybody else."

"Anybody can join," said the boy, whose name, Matt recalled, was Robert. Turning back to Matt, he added, "You should come out with us."

Matt nodded, then continued to copy the last sentence from the board.

"We call it the 100-Kilometre Club," said Robert. "And it's kind of fun."

Ryan rose, ignoring the look Ms. Wellesley was giving him. "Fun? Maybe if you ran faster, Maxwell, it might be more *fun*. I wonder where our new coach is?"

Matt finished his notes and closed his book. From her seat, Ms. Wellesley had completed rearranging her files and had tidied up her desk. She looked down at Robert, who had taken the seat in front of Matt.

"I take it you are all here for the running club," she said.

"All but the new kid," said Ryan, looking at Matt. "We don't need him. Boy, I wish our coach would show up."

Ms. Wellesley hobbled over and sat on top of a student desk with her feet on the seat. "I'm your new coach," she said.

"You?" said Ryan.

"Me," she repeated. "Tonight I just wanted to get an idea of who is interested."

"Just us," said Ryan. "I'm the captain, and Baz Amin is the other runner. He's not here today. And then for the girls there's Ashley Grovier and Kathryn Lau."

"We can speak for ourselves," said the girl with the black pony tail.

"Oh, so *sorry*, Kathryn," Ryan replied sarcastically.

The door opened and Gavin Richards barged in, banging the door against the wall. "Am I late?" he asked. "For running?"

"You're in the right place," said Ms. Wellesley, smiling.

"We're not including the little kids, too, are we?" asked Ryan. "I thought this was about the cross-country team."

"We count, too," said Gavin. "Even if there is only me."

The girl with the red hair band looked up from her pencil box. "Just don't get in our way," she said.

"Sure Ashley," said Ryan. "You're the speedster all right."

So her name is Ashley, Matt thought to himself. But it was a boy's name she painted on the pencil box. She held up the box, blew on the paint to speed drying, and examined it at arm's length. Satisfied, she shook the red band from her hair. She noticed Matt looking at her and stared back with a mild smile until Matt looked away, a blush rising to his temples.

Ryan rose as though he wanted to look taller. "Last year Baz and I ran for the boys and Ashley and Kathryn for the girls," he said. "We were only in Grade Seven then. We can run again at Ganaraska Forest this year."

"Nobody else was interested," said Kathryn. "Nobody else would run."

Ms. Wellesley raised her hands. "Wait a minute, everybody. First of all, this is just a short meeting to introduce ourselves. Ryan Abolins, Ashley Grovier, Kathryn Lau and Matt Thompson are in my class," she said, nodding at each as she said their names. She looked at Gavin. "And what is your name?"

"My name is Gavin Richards, and I'm the fastest kid in Grade Four."

"My name is Ms. Wellesley, and I sprained my ankle last week so I'm not very fast at all. I'm pleased to meet you, Gavin."

Ryan half laughed, half snorted, and pulled at the rings in his left ear.

Ms. Wellesley continued. Matt found himself listening, even though he had completed his work and packed his backpack.

"There are two goals for this club," she said. "Of course, as Ryan has said, we want the school to do well at the district cross-country meet. But before that, we want to encourage as many students as possible to come out and join us for the club runs. Running is more than just racing."

"We'll meet Tuesdays and Thursdays, like last year," said Ryan. "We'll burn everybody off pretty quick."

"We'll meet every night," said Ms. Wellesley, slowly, "right after 3:30 dismissal."

"Every night?" said Ryan.

"Every night."

"What if I can't make it every night?" He flicked an elastic band that landed in Kathryn's hair.

"I have music lessons on Wednesday nights," said Ashley.

"I go out to the stables on Mondays, Wednesdays and Fridays," said Kathryn, shaking her ponytail until the elastic fell out.

Ms. Wellesley continued. "And I have meetings on some nights, and won't be able to make it. But otherwise, we run every night. If you want to be fit, you have to run almost every day."

Ashley closed her pencil box. "Last year Mr. Janzen said once a week was fine. He kept track of our laps, and anybody who ran enough to make up 100 kilometres got an award. Are we going to do that again?"

"That's a very good idea," said Ms. Wellesley. "The 100-Kilometre Club. How many of you finished the 100 kilometres?"

Ryan, Robert, Ashley, and Kathryn all raised their hands.

"Baz did, too. But we were the only ones," said Kathryn. "Everybody else quit."

"I didn't quit," said Gavin. "It was just too far. But I'll do it this year."

Ms. Wellesley smiled. "But 100 kilometres, that's a lot of laps. I didn't know you had a track."

The others laughed, but Matt didn't see what was funny. He had finished his work. He didn't know why he stayed at the meeting.

"We don't," said Ryan. "We run around the block, down Centrefield Street and back on Varcoe."

"How far is that?"

"Mr. Janzen said it was 2.2 kilometres," said Kathryn. "But to get the award you had to run fifty laps."

Ms. Wellesley said, "So we'll call it the 100-Kilometre Club again," she said. "One of our jobs will be to encourage more people to join."

"Whadda we want to do that for?" groaned Ryan. "It's just to pick the fastest runners for the cross-country meet at Ganaraska. And we know who that is. Baz and me."

Kathryn brightened. "It'll be easier to get to 100 kilometres if I can run three times a week. Maybe sometimes we can run two or three laps."

Ms. Wellesley smiled at her. "I hope so. The school cross-country race will be in October …"

"You mean Harriers?" asked Kathryn.

"Harriers is an old English term for fox hunting," said Ms. Wellesley. "A long time ago runners made up a game, pretending they were hounds running after foxes. That became cross-country running."

Ashley looked up from her pencil box. "Cool," she said.

"That's a waste," said Ryan, bristling. "Why get a whole bunch of people to run when we need only two guys and two girls for Ganaraska? Baz'll be here tomorrow. So it'll be Baz and me, Ashley and Kathryn. There's your team." He leaned back and smiled.

"First," said Ms. Wellesley, "we want to encourage everyone to run. Secondly, maybe there are some faster people this year. Matt, here, is new to the school. Maybe he wants to run."

"Oh, yeah, right," said Ryan, crossing his arms. "I'll beat him any day."

Matt felt a flash of anger. Back in London, he had not been the fastest runner in his school. Hockey was his favourite sport. But last year he had finished third in the 1500-metre race at the school field day.

"Anyway," said Ms. Wellesley, spreading her hands, "that's it for tonight. First run will be tomorrow night. And let's talk it up and get lots of runners out. And Ryan, don't forget that the principal wants to see you."

As the students left the room, Ms. Wellesley looked over at Matt. "I'm new to this school, too," she said. "I hope you'll join us."

Matt looked up at Ms. Wellesley, then looked at Ryan's departing back.

He said nothing.

* * *

After dinner that night, Catherine-Marie flounced down the stairs and slammed a book on the dining room table at which Matt should have been doing his homework.

"You've been in my room!" she shouted.

Matt looked up, wordless.

"Now where's my novel? You took—"

"I didn't take nothing."

"There, you admit it. Mom, make him give it back."

Mrs. Thompson emerged from the den on the lower floor. "What's going on?"

"He took my book," she said, much too loudly. "He's been sneaking around in my room!"

"Have you, Matt?"

"No. And I didn't take nothing."

"Didn't take anything."

"Whatever."

"Your father will be home shortly. I have a lot of work to finish up. You'd think you were both preschoolers."

"Just tell him to stay out," said Catherine-Marie, stomping back up the stairs. She slammed her door.

"Whatever you were doing, don't do it," said Mrs. Thompson, retreating back into the den, closing the door behind her.

"I didn't …"

Matt found himself alone at 8:00 on a Tuesday night.

5

The Runners Meet

Twenty-four students gathered in the school foyer the next day. They fidgeted, stretched, yawned, and blinked, all under the watchful eyes of the six former school principals who stared down at them from framed photographic portraits.

Matt hung around the edge of the foyer. He hadn't really decided to turn out for the running club, but hadn't decided not to either. The new school had not thrilled him. So far, only teachers and the principal had talked to him. And Robert, once. He didn't count Ashley's smiles.

"Hey look!" said Ryan, spotting him. "It's the new guy. Don't tell me you really think you can run?" Ryan had shed his fashionable pants and shirt for running shorts, a T-shirt, and almost-new shoes with untied laces.

"Don't pay any attention to him," said Kathryn, her ponytail swishing as she turned to Matt. "Ryan just doesn't like competition."

"What competition?" replied Ryan. "I don't see no competition. Baz, do you see competition?"

Baz Amin was Matt's height, with dark, glistening hair and dark, fierce eyes. He looked at Matt and smiled. "Back off, Abolins," he said. "Do your boasting on race day." Matt knew then that Baz was the one to beat, not Ryan.

"Come on, run with us," said Robert. His white T-shirt and red shorts had been ironed smooth. The shorts even had a crease. "It'll be fun."

"Too bad about old Janzen," said another girl who Matt didn't recognize.

"Oh, yeah, Janzen," said Ryan. "The lap counter. As if runners need a coach. So where is our new *coach*, eh? We gotta get going. Maybe I'll go into the staff room and get her." Ryan laughed. Everyone knew the staff room was off limits.

"You know, Ryan," said Kathryn, "it's the first day and we have six weeks or more before racing. Besides, you haven't been named captain this year."

"Gawk!" piped in Ashley, shaking out her hair and tying it with an orange hair band. "I mean, let's get this over. I'm supposed to meet my boyfriend, Sean, right after school, so I can't stand around and wait." Ashley wore basketball shorts that came down to her knees, high socks that almost reached her knees, and a stylish sweater that said "University of Ontario Institute of Technology" on the front.

Matt noticed that half the runners were from the junior grades. Of these, he recognized only one. Gavin jumped up and down. "I'm running today, too," he said. "My dad said I would get new running shoes for races." He bounced up and down, the broken shoelaces of his worn old shoes flapping.

Matt moved to the corner and tried to look inconspicuous. Ryan thrust a finger at him. "Hey, new kid," he said. "This is the cross-country team. You better not hang around." He laughed and looked around at the others. Everybody laughed politely except for Kathryn and Robert.

"I can run," Matt said, thinking that Ryan, with his orange hair and rings in his ears, looked like a Popsicle with medals.

"Yeah, I'll bet," said Ryan. "We run fast here. Don't get in our way. Besides, you sure don't look dressed to run."

Matt didn't. He had worn jeans and golf shirt to school, and his shoes were scuffed from a summer of fun. His mother had bought him new back-to-school shoes that he had not worn on purpose.

"You don't look like much yourself, Ryan," Kathryn interjected.

Ryan looked up at the clock and headed toward the front door of the school. "That's enough for me," he said. "Come on, you guys. Let's get this show on the road."

Ryan led the parade of runners out the front door. Robert stayed in the foyer. Kathryn kept looking down the hall for the missing teacher.

"I really think we should wait," she said.

"Then wait," said Ryan over his shoulder.

Matt watched as the runners walked around the school buses at the front entrance. At the sidewalk, Ryan, Ashley and then Baz broke into a flat-out run. The younger runners followed.

Robert and Kathryn came out the front door and exchanged glances. Kathryn shrugged.

"I'll wait with you," Robert said.

Matt watched the runners disappearing down the sidewalk. He was irked by Ryan's attitude, but pleased that at least two people had spoken to him.

"We're going to wait for Ms. Wellesley," Robert said. "She said she would be here."

"I'll wait, too," said Matt. "I didn't bring my running clothes today."

When he uttered the sentence, he realized he had made a decision about the running club. He stood with Robert and Kathryn. The last of the junior runners disappeared around the corner a long block away at Centrefield Street.

"Oh, dear!" Ms. Wellesley stood with a clipboard resting on her hip. "Have they left already?"

"About a minute ago," said Robert.

"I wanted to meet with everyone and talk about what we hope to do this year," the teacher said, gazing down the empty sidewalk. "We didn't get off to a very good start, did we?"

She limped toward them. A seventh-grade girl followed her.

Robert turned. "That announcement at noon brought out a lot of new runners."

"And they're all out running on the streets and I don't even know who all's out there," said Ms. Wellesley. Her voice sounded flat, as though she were disappointed in herself.

"But we've got a lot of people interested, and that's good," she said, perking up. "Now let's see if I've got everybody's name right." To the Grade Seven student she nodded. "We've never met. Your name?" She wrote down the name — Hannah Singh. "And I know Kathryn." She wrote her name on the clipboard.

"And Robert. Do you prefer Rob or Robbie instead?"

Robert looked at this new teacher and swallowed. "Uh, Robert," he said after hesitating. "Just Robert."

"And Matt. Good to see you here, Matt." Name scribbled down.

"So how many runners do we have out today?"

Kathryn answered. "About a dozen or so. Baz, Jason, Ryan, Ashley — they're the leaders. They'll likely be back first. Then the rest."

"Whatever prompted them to run off like that?" asked Ms. Wellesley.

Robert shrugged. "Last year our coach, Mr. Janzen, came out just to keep track of who was here and write down the names of everybody who ran a lap. We started when we wanted."

Ms. Wellesley raised an eyebrow. "You guys ran on your own without coaching? Just running laps? No wonder most quit."

"Well, Mr. Janzen said he had never run before. Two years ago Mr. Deans used to run with us, but he retired."

"Kids running without being coached — that's a sign of strong motivation. I can see we've got the building blocks for a great team. And how did you do last year?"

Robert looked down at his left toe. "Jason was fifth at the districts at Ganaraska. He's in high school now. And Kathryn here was fourth."

"And you?"

Robert Maxwell looked up when he answered. "I was fourth in Harriers in the school meet. Only the top three got to go to Ganaraska."

"I can see we've got a lot of good talent to work with. Well, are you ready to run today?"

All four nodded.

"Unfortunately, this leg will keep me here for now," Ms. Wellesley said.

"Is it bad?" asked Kathryn, never afraid to ask a question that might be none of her business.

"It's a minor sprain, but I'm not supposed to run on it for a few days," Ms. Wellesley replied. "I'll stay here and meet the others on their way in. You guys could head off now. And take it easy, eh? Keep together, run relaxed."

Ms. Wellesley watched as they started off down the sidewalk in front of the school.

In spite of the teacher's advice, all were running hard by the time they reached the edge of the school grounds. Matt shifted uncomfortably, wishing he was dressed to run with them.

Ms. Wellesley stood on the tarmac at the entrance to the small school parking lot, clasping her clipboard and waiting for the return of the runners. A few cars turned into the drive, as parents picked up children. The Canadian flag flapped from the flagpole. The custodian worked on hands and knees in a flower bed. Matt recognized him from his adventure on the portable roof.

The teacher turned to Matt. "I think we've got our work cut out to build a team here," she said, as though he were an old friend. "Tomorrow, bring your running gear, do you hear?"

Matt nodded, and began to wonder what kind of gear he needed.

* * *

"Shoes."

The clerk in the running store had a badge that said "Running Gear Coach." Mrs. Thompson, stunned by the answer, simply repeated it. "Shoes?"

The Running Gear Coach looked at Matt. "The only necessary equipment for running is shoes," he said. "Run without shoes or in bad shoes, and sooner or later you'll get hurt. All the rest is optional. However, we do suggest at least shorts." He smiled. "In winter you might want to wear even more."

How different from hockey, where every piece of equipment was necessary — and expensive!

"Eventually, we can sell you shorts and shirts and jackets and special clothing, especially if you want to run all year." The clerk, only slightly taller than Mrs. Thompson, was lean, fit, and wore the weather on his face. "But all you really need is shoes."

"Socks?" added Mrs. Thompson.

"I can sell you some, but they can be any socks as long as they're in good shape."

"Shorts?"

"As long as they don't restrict movement. Matt's likely more interested in wearing what the others wear than what competitive runners wear."

Another difference, Matt thought. In hockey everyone wanted the same equipment worn by a favourite star.

With the clerk's help they picked out a pair of shoes. Matt tried them on, walked back and forth across the store. He liked the feel of the cushioned soles.

"Cross-country?" asked the clerk. Matt nodded.

"You might want these." He pulled down a pair with mean-looking black rubber knobs on the soles. "Better traction, especially if it rains, which in October and November it's likely to do. And you need lateral support, because on rough ground you can go over on your ankle easily enough."

"Run in the rain?" Matt asked.

"Cross-country? Sure. You're not a lump of sugar. You're not going to dissolve in the rain."

"But wouldn't it get slippery in the mud?"

"Rain, sleet, ice, mud," said the clerk with smile. "That's part of the thrill of cross-country. Think of the soles of your shoes as mud tires."

The fourth pair of shoes fit perfectly and felt good. Matt refused an offer to try them in a run along the sidewalk in front of the strip mall.

"Who's your coach?" asked the clerk as Mrs. Thompson was paying for the shoes.

"Ms. Wellesley," said Matt. "My teacher."

"Fran Wellesley? How's her ankle? Heard she had a bit of a problem a few weeks ago. Anyway, good luck. Don't let a little mud scare you."

6

The Crunch of Toast

The next day, despite her promise to arrive right after the dismissal, Ms. Wellesley was late again. The runners met in the lobby. Ryan did a windmill with alternate arms, and headed for the door.

"Let's go, everybody," he said. "Gotta get this over with."

Ryan plunged ahead, pushing open the school door with his foot. Like lemmings, the other runners, old and young alike, followed him.

Matt had been at the far corner of the lobby, near the gym door. Dressed in his new running shoes, a pair of old shorts, and a T-shirt, he felt that at least he now fit in.

But his idea of racing head-to-head with Ryan evaporated as Ryan led the runners outside. Matt tried to follow, but the runners mixed in with other students burdened with backpacks. The students got wedged in the doorway like a stubborn cork. By the time Matt got to the parking lot, the runners were strung out along the sidewalk as far as he could see. Ryan, Ashley, Baz — all the senior runners except Kathryn and Robert — were out of sight.

Kathryn said, "We're going to wait for Ms. Wellesley."

Matt looked first at Kathryn, then at Robert, then back at the string of runners.

"I'm going to catch up," he said, and bounded across the parking lot, over the boulevard to the sidewalk, his new shoes full of energy.

His efficient stride helped him easily catch the first group of younger runners. After about 300 metres, at the first corner, he picked his way through and around others. Within two minutes he had covered 400 metres, and had passed more than a dozen runners.

Many runners had started out too fast and had already stopped to walk. Matt powered on. He was beginning to breathe more deeply. He wished he had started out with Ryan and the lead group.

The younger runners were all behind him now. He could see three, perhaps four runners ahead. By the second mailbox he caught Ashley. Her green hair band had come undone. She had slowed to a jog, but even that looked difficult. She was gasping for breath.

As Matt moved to pass her, she waved. "Hey, hi! Isn't this awful?"

Matt waved as he went by. Ahead, Ryan pounded along in untied shoes. Matt was gaining on him.

The sidewalk looped through a residential subdivision, then turned past an undeveloped wooded area. Halfway along this long back stretch, Ryan turned and saw Matt a car-length back. Immediately he sped further ahead, changing from the survival jog to a hard run, stretching the distance between them.

Matt continued, his breath deep. His arms and legs grew heavy. He focused on the back of Ryan's shirt, aimed at it like a target, as Ryan settled into an even pace 20 metres ahead.

By the turn onto Varcoe Street, Matt had cut the gap between himself and Ryan in half; 10 metres, 8, 6. Again, laces flapping, Ryan glanced over his shoulder. A half-block ahead,

Matt could see Baz running with ease, his black hair glistening in the late summer sunshine.

Matt pulled up close enough to Ryan to see individual strands of orange hair. Ryan sped up again, increasing the distance between them to 8, 10, 12 metres. Matt tried this time to catch him, but his legs wouldn't co-operate. Each step had become heavy, his breath in gulping gasps.

Past the fourth mailbox and around the corner the course continued, the last 100 metres on a slight grade. At the parking lot, Matt pulled in, a half-dozen strides behind Ryan. He dropped to the grass, gasping, sucking air as though he could never get enough.

"Man, I'm outta shape!" Ryan said, bent over, his hands on his knees.

"Eleven minutes!" said Baz, consulting his sports watch. "That's as good as last year. Not bad!"

He looked down at Matt, nodded, turned to Ryan.

"The new kid thought for a while he was going to pass me," Ryan said.

"Looks like he did not bad."

"He only thinks he can run. As long as he knows who's captain."

Ms. Wellesley approached, armed with her clipboard. "Hi. We missed at the beginning again. You guys ran hard."

Ryan ran his hand through his hair, tugged at the rings in his ear. "Baz and I are the captains."

Ms. Wellesley looked at him strangely. "Well, as last year's captains you can help me set up for this year," she said. "It'll take a few days for me to get to know everybody." She turned and found herself surrounded by runners.

"From now on," she said, "no one leaves for the run until I have arrived and know you're out there. It's too dangerous."

"You mean we have to wait?" asked Ryan, an edge to his voice.

"I promise I'll be quicker off the mark from now on. But it's one thing everyone must do," she said. "Everyone stays put until I arrive."

"Aww," said Ryan, ready to argue.

"Everyone," repeated the teacher, firmly.

She turned her attention to two younger runners coming up the sidewalk.

Matt looked back at the school. Tony Tuchuck was once again digging among the flowers that had survived the summer. As Ryan and Baz walked by, the custodian straightened for a moment and wiped his brow with his sleeve.

"New kid's gonna give you a run for it this year," Matt could hear him say.

Ryan glanced in Matt's direction. "Forget it, Tony," he said with a sneer. "He's toast."

"He didn't look like toast to me. Where'd he catch you?"

"He didn't," Ryan said. "And he won't."

"Oh," Mr. Tuchuk said. Then, "Well, Ryan, you had a full minute, maybe more, on him at the start, but he was right on your tail at the end." Matt glanced back after the others had turned away. The custodian looked up and winked at him.

* * *

Matt's father was surprised, perhaps even pleased, but Matt could not tell for sure. "Cross-country?" his father asked. "You're running cross-country?"

Matt shrugged. "I went out for the running club. We run around the block. Cross-country is later, maybe after Thanksgiving. We run a school race and the top three go to the districts.

I want to do something."

"Cross-country is good," he said. "It would give …" His voice trailed off as the kitchen phone rang. "I hope that's not someone at work," he said.

"Mom already took me to buy shoes," Matt said, trying to regain his father's attention.

Matt's mother came in from the garden. "Was that the phone?" she asked.

The phone rang again. "Don't answer it," said Mr. Thompson. "If it's someone from work, I'll call back."

He turned back to Matt. "What?" he said.

"S'okay," said Matt.

"Cross-country. Good for cardio, you know, heart and lungs, endurance. Get you in shape for …" He paused. Matt knew he was going to say "hockey."

"Danny Smith from work left a message for you," Mrs. Thompson said as she entered the family room. "He wants you to go back to work tonight to finish up that project. Somebody or other goofed off again."

"Drat," said Mr. Thompson quietly.

Matt flicked on the TV, but as usual there was nothing on.

7

The Coach Runs

The runners who met after school on Monday looked tired. A few drops of rain, like the drift from a lawn sprinkler, dampened their cheeks.

"Let's hurry up," said Ryan. "Let's go before it rains."

"Yeah, come on, Ms. Wellesley," said Kathryn. "I have to muck out stalls tonight."

"Just wait up, everybody," said Gavin. "Ms. Wellesley will be here soon."

"Yeah, yeah, yeah," said Ryan. "I can't wait any longer. Anyone else coming? We'll do one lap and burn it."

"But she said …"

"Do you think I care what she says?" snapped Ryan. "We ran well before she decided to be a coach. We don't need her."

"Want me to go in the staff room and get her?" asked Gavin.

"You better not, Gavy," said Ashley. "You'll get in lots of trouble."

"I do want to get going," said Hannah. "But I'll wait."

"It's, like, going to pour," said Ashley, adjusting her green hair band. "I'll get my hair all messed up and everything. Besides," she added, "I have to meet my boyfriend, Karl."

"Let's do it, then," said Ryan. "Who's coming?" He started to move, a tentative shuffle at first. Baz and Ashley followed, and then two or three of the younger runners.

Matt stood and watched. Already Baz and Ryan were running hard, with Ashley close behind. Matt wanted to run with them, to run until his lungs burned to show he could beat them. He was about to follow them when Tony Tuchuk straightened up from the flower bed.

"Some of you guys are too impatient," he said.

"Give her some time," said Robert. "She's likely giving some clown a detention."

"We're the clowns in her class," said Matt. "I don't remember any detentions."

"She did say she'd be here," said Kathryn.

"She's coming now," said Matt. "It looks as though she's dressed to run."

"Now, aren't you glad you waited?" asked Tony Tuchuk.

Ms. Wellesley crossed the corner of the parking lot and walked toward them, her head slightly bowed as though she were looking for pennies. She had her hair pulled back in a ponytail. She wore a T-shirt, nylon shorts, and a new pair of running shoes.

"Sorry I'm late," she said. "I had to change."

Gavin bounded up and down, up and down in the same spot. "Are you going to run, Ms. Wellesley?" he asked. "Are you going to run with us today?"

Ms. Wellesley smiled. "I think I would like that, Gavin," she said. "Is everybody here?"

"Some of them didn't wait," replied Robert.

"Oh, dear. Well, we're not going to catch them. But maybe with practice I can change fast enough to get out here before they take off next time," Ms. Wellesley replied.

"Are you really going to run?" asked Gavin. "Do you want me to teach you?"

"I don't think that's necessary," Ms Wellesley replied.

"Everybody set? Let's go."

She started jogging across the parking lot to the sidewalk. "And remember," she added, "everybody stay together. We're not racing."

She led the group, jogging easily, down the sidewalk.

"What about stretches and stuff?" asked Hannah. "You didn't do stretches."

"Warm-up is more important," replied the coach. "Stretching before you run is not the best time. It's better to stretch at the end of a run."

"That's backwards," said Hannah.

"If you stretch when your muscles are warm, they stretch further. You won't be stiff and sore next day."

"I could run like this all day," said Gavin. "Betcha I could run a marathon."

"Maybe. But a marathon would take us five hours or so, jogging like this," said Ms. Wellesley. "A marathon is 42 kilometres and almost 200 metres long — that's 26 miles, 385 yards. Unless you trained for it, you wouldn't make it."

"Wow!"

"One of Canada's best marathon runners ever came from Clarington."

"Who was that?" asked Matt.

"Her name was Sylvia Ruegger. Her best marathon time from 1985 is still the fastest ever run by a Canadian woman," Ms. Wellesley replied.

"How fast?"

"Two hours, 28 minutes, and 36 seconds," the teacher replied.

"That's a long time," Gavin said.

"That's also fast. At the speed she was running you would finish this loop in seven and a half minutes."

"Even Baz takes more than ten minutes!" said Robert.

"It's fast," said Ms. Wellesley. "Believe me, it's fast."

"And she went to high school here?" asked Kathryn.

"Clarke High School," Ms. Wellesley replied. "She was my hero when I was in high school. The first marathon she ever ran is the fastest first marathon by any woman. Ever. In the world. Period."

"I'll bet she set every record at school."

"She started out running cross-country in the seventh grade because she always got beaten in the sprints."

When they reached the mailbox that marked half-way, Kathryn moved up to Ms. Wellesley's shoulder. "Are we going to jog the whole loop like this?" she asked.

"You're in a hurry."

"I do have to go to the stables after."

"But don't get hurry sickness."

"Huh?"

Ms. Wellesley stopped running and stepped onto the grass on the boulevard between the sidewalk and the street.

"Gather around," she said as stragglers drew up.

"But we're supposed to go all the way around."

"We will. Now that we're warmed up, I'll show you a little exercise. And a bit of stretch."

Ms. Wellesley demonstrated the big lunge: one leg out behind, the other at a 90-degree angle in front of her. "Just hold that for a slow count of twenty," she said. "Carefully. Never bounce when you stretch. Good. Now, we're going to do some surges."

"Some what?" asked Matt.

"Kathryn wants to run a bit faster. We're going to do that."

"How?"

"Follow my lead," she said. "We're going to surge, but only while we count out fifty left feet. Then we slow to a jog again. Got it?"

Heads nodded.

"Let's … do it!"

Ms. Wellesley bounded ahead with easy long strides. Matt struggled, trying to keep up. The first few steps were easy. Then he had to work harder. Beside him, Kathryn grunted. Behind them, he could hear Robert's heavy step.

"Forty-eight, forty-nine, fifty …"

Ms. Wellesley dropped back to an easy jog, still breathing lightly. The runners slapped forward, some panting.

"An easy jog for two minutes and we'll do that again."

Matt jogged beside the teacher. He recovered his breath quickly. "That wasn't too hard," he said.

"Good training often isn't. Try to keep that up for 2 kilometres and it'll be different. That's called racing. But in training, we'll just run at that pace for seventy-five left feet, then one hundred."

"Like carrying the calf," said Robert from behind.

"What d'ya mean?" asked Gavin, panting.

"I read about a guy who carried a calf every day when it was small. After a year, he was still lifting the calf every day, but the calf was full-grown."

"Progressive training works," said Ms. Wellesley.

She turned to the group. "One more surge today," she said. "Kathryn, you lead this time."

"Me?"

"In a good team, we take turns leading the surges. Everybody ready? Then let's do it — now!"

Kathryn darted ahead at a faster pace. Matt pushed up beside her, began to pass.

"Let Kathryn lead," said Ms. Wellesley from the back of the pack. "You'll get a chance."

The group jogged back to the school. Ryan, Baz, and Ashley were lounging in the parking lot. If they thought it at all unusual that Ms. Wellesley was running, they did not show it.

"So, did you guys go around twice?" asked Ryan. "You took long enough."

"We ran fast!" shouted Gavin.

"In the time you were gone, we could have run the whole loop twice," said Ryan. To Ms. Wellesley he said, "Put me down for one lap. Maybe next time I'll do two."

Ms. Wellesley turned. "Ryan and Ashley. And Baz Amin. I want to see all of you over here for a moment." She walked to the end of the parking lot.

"Uh-oh," said Gavin. "You guys are going to get it."

Ryan exchanged glances with the others and shrugged.

"Now!" said Ms. Wellesley. "The three of you." Reluctantly they followed to a spot just out of earshot. Matt could see Ryan attempting an explanation. Ms. Wellesley didn't raise her voice, but twice, three times she held up a hand, then finished the conversation with a horizontal slashing movement with both hands.

"I think they got told to not start off on their own," said Kathryn.

Matt watched as Ryan slouched back past the flagpole to where Baz was standing. Mr. Tuchuk pointed his gardening trowel.

"Looks like you've got a real coach this time," Matt heard him say.

"Wellesley? Naw. She's bought the shoes, looks like, but doesn't know how to use them," Ryan replied. "And what'd I say? That new kid didn't even try to keep up today."

The custodian smiled. "That new coach knows a lot about running. She just needs to learn how to convince you."

"Yeah, right," said Ryan.

"Well," said Mr. Tuchuk. "You'll see."

8

Something Wrong

The light from the TV flickered like a dying fire. Matt slouched on the sofa, eyes fixed but not really seeing. From the top of the stairs, his sister called.

"Turn that thing down!" she yelled. "I can't hear myself think."

Matt pulled himself from his daydream of beating Ryan in the school championships. He looked at the TV and saw an image of Terry Fox doing his shuffling run, heading toward the sunset on a hill near Thunder Bay. The sound was low and could barely be heard.

"It's down now, for goodness sake," he called up the stairs.

"I can't study. It's driving me crazy."

"Maybe you're already there," replied Matt. "I just hope it's not genetic."

"You, you …" Catherine-Marie halted, her thoughts so far ahead of her tongue that she could say nothing.

The den door opened, and their mother emerged frowning. "What on earth is going on here?" she asked. "I've got a deadline to meet, and with you two yelling and screaming—"

"It's Matt," said Catherine-Marie. "He's got that TV so loud you can hear it down the block."

"I have not! She's just—"

"Hold it, hold it," said their mother. "Whatever is on the TV is nothing compared to what you two are doing. Now rewind and start over."

"It's the TV," said Catherine-Marie. "Make him turn it down or turn it off."

"Matt?"

"It's not loud. Is that loud? It's her — she needs earplugs."

Mrs. Thompson looked at Catherine-Marie. "It doesn't seem that loud," she said. "Now."

"He turned it down."

"Didn't."

"Did."

"Stop it, both of you. Work it out. I've got to have this news release ready for tomorrow morning. Give me some peace and quiet."

"When will Dad be home?" asked Matt.

Mrs. Thompson looked at her watch. "It's 9:30. He should be home soon."

"But the TV!" persisted Catherine-Marie.

Mrs. Thompson put her hand on her left hip. "Were you really watching that, Matt?" she asked.

"Not really. That's why I had the sound turned down so I couldn't hear it. So *nobody* could hear it," he said, raising his voice for Cathy-Marie's benefit.

Mrs. Thompson retreated into the den. "You two screaming at each other. Your father working all hours. There's something wrong with this."

Matt flicked the TV off as the den door closed. *And a mother barricaded in her office*, he thought, and too late wished he had said it out loud.

Upstairs, Catherine-Marie slammed her bedroom door.

9

Peppermint's Pandemonium

The next afternoon, Kathryn brought her pet rat for a demonstration in science class. A hooded rat with a collar, Peppermint came in a wire cage.

"Mr. Dunbarton isn't here this afternoon, so you can take that slimy animal home," Ashley said when she saw Kathryn arrive. "We're going to get Mrs. MacMillan, I bet. Or a supply. I hope we get out early. I've got to meet my new boyfriend."

"We're supposed to have a time trial this afternoon at running club," Kathryn replied.

"That's tomorrow afternoon."

"Who's the lucky guy this time, Ashley?" asked Robert. Ashley sat at her desk with a small bottle of whiteout, covering the names of former boyfriends and then painting on the name of her newest boyfriend. The pencil box was thick with paint and whiteout.

"I think Matt is cute," Ashley replied, looking up. Matt blushed.

Kathryn turned from the rat cage. "You think everybody's cute," she said.

"Well, aren't they?" Ashley blew on the whiteout gingerly

to hasten the drying.

Ryan sauntered into the room just as the first bell rang. "Hey! Some rat cage!" he said. He looked at Kathryn, "That yours?"

"Her name's Peppermint."

"She bite?"

"Look." She reached into the cage, pulled out the rat, and placed it on her right shoulder. "She'll ride up there all day."

"Cool." Ryan reached out with a tentative finger, moving it close to the rat's nose. The rat sniffed nervously, then reached up with a tiny paw and touched his knuckle.

"Eww! Get that thing away from me!" said Ashley, backing away. "It's gross!"

"I'm going out to get a drink before the final bell," said Ryan. Matt followed him out the door, meaning to hang up his jacket.

Mrs. MacMillan stood in the hallway just outside the classroom door.

"The bell's gone, people," she said. "Just because your regular teacher's not here is no reason to be late."

Ryan grunted. As he approached the heavy, reinforced glass doors to the main foyer he raised his foot, pressed against the metal plate around the door handle, and pushed hard.

"Ryan Abolins, come here," the principal said, quietly but firmly.

Ryan turned, his face a mask.

"Is that the proper way to open a door?" she asked.

"It's quicker."

"Can you think of any reason that might not be appropriate behaviour?"

Ryan looked up at the principal and sighed. That was her favourite phrase, "appropriate behaviour."

"It shouldn't matter …"

"Ryan, if someone had been coming the other way, you could have injured them."

Ryan glanced through the glass doors. He looked back at Mrs. MacMillan, who stood firmly with her hands on her hips.

"Well?"

Ryan dropped his eyes. "I'm sorry. I didn't mean it," he said. But he sounded as though he did.

Mrs. MacMillan stepped aside and let both him and Matt back into the classroom.

The students shuffled to their seats. Mrs. MacMillan introduced the supply teacher for the afternoon, then left.

During the next hour, the supply teacher tried to follow the lesson plan Mr. Dunbarton had provided, but with little success. About a half-hour into the lesson, Kathryn turned to check on her pet.

"Peppermint's out!" she said, darting to the back of the room. "Somebody opened the cage! We've got to find her!"

The classroom turned to uproar. Students left their desks and began the hunt for the missing rat, some dropping to their knees to look under shelves, others standing on tiptoes to peek on top. Ashley Grovier searched by standing on her desk.

"People! People! People!" said the supply teacher. "Everyone sit down. Now."

No one paid attention.

"Desks, now, or I'll give a class detention at recess."

No one, not even the supply teacher, knew if it was possible to give the whole class a detention. Few wanted to pursue the challenge to find out.

The students settled in their seats. "Right. Now why don't we all write down our notes on this science lesson," said the teacher. "We have time before recess."

The class settled somewhat as everyone rummaged in desks

for notebooks and pencils.

Matt happened to be watching as Ashley bent to get her pencil box from her desk. She held it for a moment in her hands. Then, with a jerk, she flung it into the air. Pencils, pens and her whiteout bottle flew in all directions.

"Eeeeeek!" screamed Ashley.

"What's the fuss?" asked Matt.

"I think she just found Peppermint," replied Kathryn.

10

A Training Game

"We're burning 'em out," Ryan said one Thursday while the club was waiting for Ms. Wellesley to appear.

"What do you mean?" asked Robert.

"Well, look," he said. "Count the runners. Almost half of the runners have dropped out. Just like I told old Wellesley that first day. Most of them aren't tough enough to run cross-country."

Matt looked around and thought that Ryan might be right. Many of the runners, those who weren't as fast, had stopped coming out after school.

"They'll come back now that they know Ms. Wellesley is running, too," said Kathryn.

"Yeah, right," said Ryan. "If you call what she does running. She's just a teacher. She thinks she can coach me? I could beat her any day."

Just then, Tony Tuchuk walked across the foyer carrying a stepladder.

"Don't be too sure," he said, loud enough that everyone heard but no one was really sure if they had.

"Whaddaya mean?" asked Ryan.

But the custodian had disappeared down the hallway toward the library.

"Well, you can do that fancy stuff with Wellesley," said Ryan.

"But Baz and me, we're training to race so we get our lap time down to ten minutes this year. And if old Wellesley shows up late again, we'll just go out on our own."

Just then Ms. Wellesley appeared, dressed in her nylon running suit and running shoes. She had solved the problem, Matt noted, by changing into her running outfit at recess.

"It's about time," said Ryan.

"You're early," said Ashley.

"I had to do something," said Ms. Wellesley. "We were starting to lose people. We have everybody now?"

Ms. Wellesley ticked off the names of a dozen runners, then put her clipboard aside.

"Today," she said, "we're going to do something different."

Outside, she led them behind the school, jogging slowly across the soccer pitch toward the park. The park was shaped like a bowl, each side sloping 2 to 3 metres to a baseball diamond.

"We gonna get laps in today, or what?" asked Ryan.

Ms. Wellesley smiled. "Today, no laps. Let's have fun."

"Will this take long?" asked Ashley. "I've got to meet Jason after."

Kathryn turned. "So? I've got to go to the stables after, too. But if we're going to run we should do it right."

"Right?" said Ryan, turning to face Ms. Wellesley. "How are we going to do it right if we don't run laps? How we gonna train then? We gotta run laps so I can do well at Ganaraska. This year we're going to win."

Ms. Wellesley smiled patiently. "Laps are wonderful for endurance," she said, "but if you want to run faster, you must run faster."

Ryan twisted his baseball cap. Matt could see anger in his face.

"We ain't gonna do those surges, are we?"

"They work."

"I don't need no jogger to show me how to run better. How're you going to show us how? I can run faster than you. How're you gonna show me?"

Ryan stared at Ms. Wellesley, who stared back for a full minute before replying.

"I'm not out here to fight and argue," she said finally. "I'm out here to encourage you, and to help you improve."

"I don't need no *coach*," said Ryan, spitting out the word.

Ryan spun around, bumping into Matt.

"Get outta my way, Thompson," Ryan snarled. "I'm gonna burn a lap. You comin', Baz? Ashley?"

Heads swiveled. Baz and Ashley moved toward Ryan. Robert and Kathryn took small steps to be closer to Ms. Wellesley. Matt stayed in the larger group in the middle.

"Running is something you do for enjoyment," said Ms. Wellesley. "Ryan, if you believe that running laps on the sidewalk will do more for you, then do it."

Ryan looked disappointed, as though he had expected a fight that he could reluctantly lose and grumble about after. He dropped his hands, defenseless.

"Okay, then, let's go," he said. He turned to jog away. Baz hesitated slightly before following him. Ashley joined them.

Matt watched the three as they jogged away. In his heart, he wanted to join them, wanted to challenge Ryan head on and show that he could beat him — if he could. Every day, Ryan still always kept ahead.

"I wonder who put vinegar on his cornflakes," Ms. Wellesley said.

She turned back to the remaining group. Matt, Robert, Kathryn, and another half-dozen runners had stayed with the coach. "When's the school Harriers?"

One of the junior runners raised a hand. "Ms. Wellesley, it's in two weeks."

"Good. Now where do you run it?"

Gavin thrust his hand in the air and spoke at the same time. "Right here!" he yelled. "Right here in the park."

Ms. Wellesley smiled. "Right. So today we're going to run in the park to get your feet, ankles, and knees used to the uneven surface.

"Running on pavement is good to teach you to run on pavement," she said. "And running slowly to finish a 2-kilometre lap is good for endurance," she added.

"But I can't run any faster than I have been," said Matt. "You mean I'm just teaching myself to run slow? I thought the surges made me faster."

"They do. But cross-country isn't run on sidewalks."

"Surges in the park?" asked Matt.

"That's the effect," said Ms Wellesley. "We play tag," she said. "The fence and the sidewalk are the boundaries, and Matt ..." Ms. Wellesley tapped Matt on the right shoulder, "*You* are it!"

She bounded away from Matt, across the park to the far fence, followed by runners of all sizes.

They played tag for a half-hour that day, panting like puppies as they chased each other. Matt and Kathryn agreed that they had never had so much fun running.

The next day his stiff muscles told him he had worked hard, too.

11

Harriers

The big day had arrived.

Two hundred and eighty-two S.T. Lovey pupils, from Grade Four to Grade Eight, lined up on a sunny fall day for the start of the school cross-country race. The winners in each division of Harriers qualified for the district finals in October at Ganaraska Forest. School rules called for everyone to take part.

Orange pylons from the custodian's supply room marked the course in the park next to the school grounds.

Junior runners went first: they ran two laps, or about 1600 metres.

Gavin, running in tattered sneakers and dirty jeans with a rip in the knee, his favourite cap askew, crossed the finish-line first.

"The champ!" he said, arms raised in victory.

"Way to go, Gavy," Ms. Wellesley said. "That was a good run."

"Yeah," said Gavin modestly, "it was."

A few minutes before the start of the race for older kids, Ms. Wellesley gathered the club runners for a final briefing.

"You have to do three laps," she said. "It's flat, there are no hills. It's about the same distance you've been running each day, but there will be one main obstacle."

"What's that?" asked Ashley, chewing her gum nervously.

"I went over this with Gavy before his race started. When you start, the course is wide. When you hit those pylons, the course narrows. You don't want to get caught in the jam."

"We sprint," said Ryan. "To get out front."

"That's right."

"That's not fair," said Kathryn. "Why couldn't they set it up so it's not so crowded?"

"It's no different at Ganaraska," said Baz. "You run the first hundred metres and there's lots of room, but when you hit trail, there's only room for about two runners."

"That's standard in cross-country," said Ms. Wellesley. "Anyway, right now you've got about five minutes before the race. Shake out the muscles, stay loose."

She looked from face to face, holding each gaze for a moment. "And good luck. This is the reason you've been training since September. All the surges you've done, running up hills here in this park. You've trained hard. Just get out there now and do your best."

Ryan looked up. "The first three go to districts, right?" he asked.

"First three each in boys and girls," Ms. Wellesley replied.

"Just checking," he said.

"He just wants to know how worried he should be," said Ashley, looking across the tarmac to Matt. Matt blushed and looked down.

* * *

When Matt tensed his muscles for the start of the cross-country race, he had only one goal: to beat Ryan.

Mr. Geisberger, the Phys. Ed. teacher, held up his hand at the far side of the schoolyard. "Ready!" he yelled. Matt and 108 other runners tensed.

"Go!" Mr. Geisberger dropped his hand.

Matt trudged forward with the crowd. Within ten steps he knew he should have started faster. Ahead, Baz and Ryan sprinted flat-out across the playground and reached the pylons ahead of everyone.

Matt was caught in a mob that wouldn't budge. His way blocked, he moved forward in tiny steps. By the time he had reached the narrow bottleneck by the pylons, he had become trapped back in the pack.

"I don't know why we have to do this," said the runner beside Matt. "I'll be lucky to finish this walking."

Slower runners blocked Matt's path. He tried sidestepping. Once he stumbled, bumped into a runner and almost fell.

Ahead, Matt could see Baz turn the first bend. Ryan was running strong in close pursuit.

Matt soon found room to dodge between and around runners. Then he broke free and began to run strongly.

At the first turn he caught Robert, then Ashley and Kathryn. He surged, passing several more runners whose quick starts had used up what little conditioning they had. Already, one or two had stopped to walk.

Matt passed several more, running confidently, his pace strong but even. By the end of the first lap he moved into third place. There was Baz, 40 metres ahead, and behind him was Ryan, half of that distance. At the turn, Matt glanced back. Robert lumbered along, 75 metres back.

The first three go to the district meet, Matt thought. For the first time he realized that he should place well enough for Ganaraska.

Running with Robert was Kathryn, her ponytail swishing behind her from side to side. Hannah followed. Behind her, Ashley gritted along, her hair band still neatly in place.

During the second lap, Matt could see Baz increasing his lead even more. And try as he might, he couldn't close the gap on Ryan.

Half-way through the third lap, Ryan suddenly appeared to be closer. Within two or three strides, the long stretch melted, and for the first time Matt could target the back of Ryan's shirt. Matt went up on his toes and kicked into a higher gear. He caught Ryan by surprise just before the final corner, enough to take a slight lead before they made the turn. It gave him the inside position, forcing Ryan to either drop back or run wide.

Ryan moved wide to gain running room. Matt pressed hard and came out of the corner a full metre ahead. They kicked through the last 50 metres, knees high and arms pumping, but Matt knew, he just knew, that this race — or at least second place — was his.

Matt crossed the finish-line running flat-out with Ryan 2 metres back. Baz, hands on his knees, greeted them with smiles. "There's our team!" he yelled, although Ryan glared at Matt and Matt looked back defiantly while all three drank air in deep swallows.

Seconds later Kathryn swept across the finish-line looking easy and relaxed. Hannah came second. Ashley, her green hair band hardly disturbed, finished third in the senior girls, side-by-side with Robert, neat, precise Robert, the two crossing the finish-line with matching strides.

"Third!" Ashley said, when she had recovered enough to talk. "I made it to the districts!"

"Fourth!" replied Robert. "Fourth! Again!" He tried to make it a joke, but there was disappointment in his eyes.

Kathryn reached out and brushed his forearm lightly. "I'm sorry," she said. "You ran well."

Matt looked across the field in time to see Ryan turn his

back on Robert and laugh. In one instant, Matt locked eyes with Robert. Matt realized he had taken the team berth that Robert wanted so dearly. Matt knew about disappointment, and recognized it in Robert's eyes.

* * *

The Thompsons had spaghetti for dinner that night. Matt thought he would always remember that.

"Well, what's new?" Matt's father asked, twirling up a forkful of noodles and rushing the cargo home before it slipped.

"We had the cross-country race today," Matt said.

"Yes, you said that was going to be today," said his mother. "That must have been great fun."

"How many ran?" asked Mr. Thompson on his second mouthful.

"The whole school," said Matt. "In our race, more than a hundred."

"Quite a mob. All at once?"

Matt nodded. "It—"

"I got my university application forms today," interrupted Cathy-Marie. "The student affairs office says we better start looking now."

"Oh my dear, I can't believe you're going to be going to university next year," said Mrs. Thompson. She dabbed at the corner of her mouth with her napkin.

"Speaking of which," said Mr. Thompson, turning to his wife. "Any luck with those prospective new clients?"

Matt's mother shook her head.

"Well, with Cathy-Marie headed for school, I'm going to need more overtime or something," he said.

"I don't like the idea of your working overtime," said Mrs.

Thompson. "We don't see you enough now."

"Maybe it would have been better if we hadn't moved," said Cathy-Marie.

"It was an opportunity," said Mrs. Thompson.

"Funny that a wife is expected to give up her job and follow her husband's career," said Cathy-Marie to her father.

"It makes sense for a family to follow the biggest salary," said Mr. Thompson. "Besides, your mother can work with her clients as well from here as in London."

"Except that some didn't think so," said Cathy-Marie. "Did you ever think of what you've asked Mother to sacrifice?"

"We've been over this before. Your mother and I talked this all over."

"I think you're very sexist!"

"Now, Cathy-Marie—"

"Don't 'now Cathy-Marie' me!" She stormed up the stairs to her bedroom.

Matt and his parents sat quietly at the table for another minute or two. Then Mr. Thompson got up and started gathering the dishes and filling the dishwasher.

"Sometimes I get the feeling we're falling apart," he said. "Whatever happened to the nice family of Thompsons who all pulled together and helped each other?"

"They lived in London," said Matt.

No one knew what to say in the silence that followed. Finally Matt's mother asked, "And how *did* you do in that race today, Matt?"

Matt shrugged. He could see no dessert was to be served.

"Okay," he said. "Just okay."

"That's nice, dear."

Matt wondered if his family would ever be the way it used to be.

12

Boy in Trouble

Matt stuffed his books in his backpack and prepared for the walk home.

"Don't forget — the district cross-country meet in Ganaraska is a week today," Ms. Wellesley said as he headed through the foyer of the school. "We want you in good shape."

"I'll be there. Though it looks as though it's going to be a matter of us all chasing Baz," he replied.

"Baz is good, and there will be other runners who are even better — remember, Baz came in sixth last year. But you are all well trained, and cross-country depends on team performance. Everybody has to run well."

"Have a good weekend, Ms. Wellesley," he said.

Matt had dawdled in the classroom. School had been dismissed a half-hour before, and now the hallway stood empty except for Tony Tuchuk, who mopped up a spilled drink. Ashley waved at Matt as he passed the library.

He left by the back door.

The tarmac area between the main school building and the portables looked lonely and deserted. An old newspaper blew across the pavement. An older man with white hair walked his dog in the park. The sun shone brightly, but the breeze nipped at his skin. Crickets sang along the fences. It was a perfect October day.

Matt walked across the school grounds. Lost in his thoughts, he almost didn't hear the voice calling him. Then, slapping footsteps rushed up behind him.

"Matt! Matt! Help us, Matt!"

A Grade Four student Matt recognized from the running club, Bradley Fishback, dashed up, turning as he reached Matt so he could half-skip, half-run backwards.

"We need you, Matt! Gavin's stuck up on the roof of a portable!"

"He's what?"

Matt turned to look. On top of the corner portable he could see a small figure, a silhouette against the sky.

"He's stuck up there and can't get down," Bradley replied. "Someone told him he would get electrocuted if he touched the wrong wire. So now he can't move!"

Matt turned and headed back to the portable. Now he could hear the sobs of the boy on the roof.

"Mike Krazowski dared him to climb up," the boy said. "Now he's up there, but some high-school guys told him he would get electrocuted if he touched the wires or the eavestrough."

"Gavin," Matt called. "Can you see me, Gavin?"

The boy on the roof peered down at Matt through half-moon eyes. Splotches of dirt covered his face. Instead of replying, he sniffled loudly, then gave a long, mournful howl, like wolf with a bellyache.

"We can't get the teachers to help him, or he'll be in real trouble," said Bradley. "That's why we need you."

Matt walked partway around the portable to get a better look. In his fear of the power lines, Gavin had wrapped his arms around the bent wooden pole that held the lines. Matt could see the pole, deadly lines and all, sway with the extra burden.

Quickly, he wriggled out of his backpack and placed it on the ground. Just as he did on Labour Day, he pulled himself onto the portable roof.

Gavin stood by the corner of the roof closest to the school. Fear had him frozen to the spot. He had begun to bawl mouthfuls of big sucking sobs.

"Here, Gavy. Give me your hand," Matt said, reaching out.

That only made the tears flow faster. "I'll die, I'll die, I'll die," howled Gavin. "Don't touch me!"

Matt looked out across the playground. He saw Ashley walking toward the park. She stopped momentarily, looked up once, then continued. Matt exhaled slowly.

The fear that paralyzed Gavin left him powerless to resist the help Matt provided. Matt reached up to pry Gavin's hands from the pole. That didn't work — Gavin clung even more tightly. Matt then held him under the arms, taking his whole weight and relieving the out-of-balance pole.

Only then did Gavin relax his grip and let Matt drag him to the corner of the roof.

"Sit down," Matt said, quietly, gently pushing the younger boy to the roof surface. Gavin folded into an awkward lump at the corner of the roof, like a puppet whose strings had been cut.

"Now we have to get you down," he said.

"No, no, no, no," repeated Gavin, sucking back sobs.

"Well, pipe down or we'll be caught," Matt said. "How did you make it up here?"

Gavin's sobs calmed a bit. Tears had etched rivers through the dirt on his face. Rather than answer, Gavin pointed to a hunk of thick yellow nylon rope that lay on the roof. Knots had been tied in it at several places so it could be used as a climbing aid.

Matt studied the rope. Deftly, he removed two of the knots and tied a loop at one end.

"Here, Gavy, pull this over your head," he said. Not waiting for Gavin to help, he pushed the loop over his head and pulled until it was snug under the boy's arms.

"You're going for a swing."

He pushed Gavin on his belly until his legs hung over the edge of the roof. Gavin looked up, his eyes wide with fear, his mouth gaping. Slowly, Matt lowered him to the stoop below.

"Okay!" yelled Bradley. "He's down now."

Matt peered over the edge to see that it was true. Gavin lay in a limp heap at the back door of the portable.

"I'm coming down!"

He dropped to the roof, pushed his legs backward over the edge and slowly lowered himself until he held his weight on his elbows. "Watch out below!" he warned. Then he lowered his weight on his arms until they were fully extended, and dropped the last half-metre.

He landed cat-like on his haunches. When he stood up, he noticed for the first time that neither Gavin nor Bradley were in sight. He locked eyes with Mrs. MacMillan.

"Matthew Thompson, we must talk. To my office. Right now!"

13

Suspended

Mrs. MacMillan said no more until Matt followed her into the office and closed the door. She gestured to a chair in front of her desk.

"I'm really disappointed, Matt," she said.

Matt dropped his eyes.

"Tell me about it," she said.

"I …" Matt didn't know how much Mrs. MacMillan had seen, had no idea where to start, or how to tell what happened without involving Gavin.

"It's not the first time, is it?" the principal asked.

Matt shook his head.

"I thought not. So tell us about these other times," she said. "Was one of those times on Labour Day weekend?"

Matt nodded.

"How're your parents going to react to this?"

Matt shrugged. His parents hadn't been interested in how he did at school, in the race, anything. Sure, they'd pay attention now. Big time. He could see being grounded for a month.

"Matt, tell me what was going on. Help me to understand."

"I can't." Matt knew he couldn't rat on Gavin. If he did, the other kids would never speak to him again.

"You realize how serious all this could be?"

Matt nodded.

"I don't think you do."

Suddenly he began to sweat — and to realize the trouble he was in.

"First, there's the danger. A fall from that height could injure you badly, perhaps even be fatal. There are power lines that could electrocute you."

"I know that."

"I suppose you do. Then there's the example. When other children see you doing something dangerous, it is likely someone else will try it. How would you feel if some younger student fell and seriously hurt himself trying to imitate you?"

"I am sorry."

"Matt, the strange thing is that I believe that. I'll give you one more chance to explain to me what this was all about."

Matt sat, elbows on his knees, eyes on the floor. He would not tell.

"Nothing? I don't know what this is all about. I do know that high-school students have been on the portable roofs. It's becoming an epidemic. It's my job to impose penalties. Now, one last time: what was this all about?"

Matt said nothing.

"Well, the school-board policy states that I have to report you. Your being on that roof gives me no choice. You are suspended from school for two days. That will likely mean you are removed from the cross-country team for Friday's meet."

She leaned back in her chair and drew her mouth into a straight line.

"Not run?" Matt said. "That's not …" Taking from him the one thing he wanted right now!

"Not fair? Tell me what's fair. Matt, I would like to find some way to understand what is going on here. Some way that would bring this incident in line with the Matthew Thompson who does so well in class. Give me some help here."

"I …" But words didn't arrive.

Mrs. MacMillan paused, held his eyes for a full minute, and then reached for the telephone.

"I'll call your parents."

14

Coming Clean

Both of Matt's parents ushered him into the house. On the short drive back from the school, no one had uttered a word.

"Cathy-Marie," Mr. Thompson called, coming in the door.

"I'm studying." The answer came from behind a closed bedroom door.

"Family conference time," said Mrs. Thompson, firmly. "We need you. Now. It's important."

Cathy-Marie emerged from her bedroom, a book in one hand. "I'm trying to make notes for an essay that's due next week," she said. "Can't it wait until dinner? And what's Dad doing home this early?"

It was 4:15. When the principal had called, both Mr. and Mrs. Thompson had been home.

"We've got a team that's working together, so I won't need to work late so often," Mr. Thompson said. "But now it's time we got this family working together again."

"But my essay—"

"Is due next week. This can't wait."

They sat at the dining-room table as though they were in a conference centre.

Mrs. Thompson looked at her daughter. "Cathy-Marie, did you know that Matt ran a cross-country race yesterday?"

Cathy-Marie pulled her eyebrows together, and said slowly, "Uh, yes." Her tone said, 'What's this got to do with anything."

"How did he do?"

"I don't know. Should I?"

"We all should have known because we are a family. And he did well; he came in second," said Mr. Thompson. "But you didn't know."

"He never told me."

"He never told us, either," said Mrs. Thompson. "We just found out today."

"Well, that isn't *my* fault."

"It's our fault," Mr. Thompson said. "Matt tried to tell us, but we were all too busy to be interested."

"I got the letter from the university—"

"Yes," said Mr. Thompson. "It was exciting for us. For you. Then you got angry at me, remember? And I was angry at the way my team at work was messing things up."

"And a couple of my clients caused me some frustration," said Mrs. Thompson. "Matt placed second in the school cross-country championship and earned a spot on the school team, and nobody paid any attention."

"That's awful," said Cathy-Marie. "I'm sorry, Matt. For not noticing."

Matt shrugged.

"Worse, now he's got into some trouble and has been suspended from school — and from the cross-country team."

"Suspended!"

"For two days."

His mother now leaned forward, one hand on Matt's arm. "Now, Matt, do you want to tell us the rest? All the stuff you wouldn't tell the principal?"

Matt did, then, tell about Gavin, and the cap back in September, and Gavin being trapped, and the rescue.

"You got there just in time," said Mrs. Thompson. "Perhaps if you were to tell Mrs. MacMillan, she would—"

"I can't, Mom," Matt said. "Gavin would be suspended and wouldn't be able to run next Friday at the Ganaraska meet."

"So you'd rather not run."

"I won't squeal."

More silence. "I can understand that," said Cathy-Marie.

Mr. Thompson cleared his throat. "Well, I can too. I told you about the team approach that we use at work. A lot of the extra hours I worked last month were because one guy kept messing up, not doing what he said he would do. And I got pretty angry. I was ready to go to my boss and have him straightened out."

"I would have done that the first time it happened," said Mrs. Thompson.

"Yes, but that's really not part of a good team approach. So I put up with it for awhile. Then — guess what happened?"

"He quit?"

"No. Everybody else was as ticked off as I was. So the whole team went to this guy and told him that he was letting a lot of other people down when he didn't show up on time or didn't complete his part of a job."

"So he's gone?"

"Nope. See, he had been resentful of me. He thought I took a job away from a good friend of his. But when he saw that what he was doing affected everybody, he changed. He took his lumps. *And* he apologized to me."

Mrs. Thompson smiled. "So what does all this have to do with Matt's problem?"

Matt looked up, and smiled at his parents for the first time in weeks.

"It means the problem is mine," Matt said. "And I'm prepared to take the lumps if I have to."

"And we're all behind you, whatever you do," said Mr. Thompson.

"But if we ever catch you on the school roof again, you'd better have an even better reason," said Mrs. Thompson with a smile as sweet as a crabapple.

* * *

On Saturday afternoon, Matt took his basketball and wandered to the schoolyard to shoot a few baskets and think. He had expected to find it deserted. But Robert and Gavin were both there, playing teammates against a non-existent foe.

"Hey, it's Matt," said Gavin.

"Hi, Matt," said Robert. "Want to shoot some baskets?"

Gavin bounced his basketball twice. "How about some one-on-two, two guys defending?"

As they set up for action, Robert asked, "So what happened yesterday? Did Mrs. MacMillan nail you?"

"Yes, she did," said Matt.

"Wow! We took off outta there pretty fast when we saw her coming. I'm sorry I didn't have any time to warn you." Gavin took the basketball, thumped it on the tarmac several times, then bounced a shot off the rim. "She give you a detention?"

"Nothing to worry about," said Matt. "I get a couple of days off school."

Robert, who had run to the brick wall to retrieve his ball, stopped in his tracks.

"You're suspended?" he asked.

"Two days."

"That's not fair!" said Gavin.

"What about Friday's meet at Ganaraska?" asked Robert.

"I can't run," Matt said.

Gavin stopped dribbling the basketball and stood with his mouth gaping. "You what?"

"You heard. I can't run in the Ganaraska race."

"That sucks," said Robert. "That really does. You're fast, and with you S.T. Lovey could win the gold."

"We won't know that, will we?"

"That's really not fair," repeated Gavin.

"Yeah, well, there it is," said Matt. "But if I can't run, Robert, then you're the next in line. You'll be able to run Ganaraska."

The smile on Robert's face glowed for a moment before fading.

"But we'll never win the gold medal with me running," he said. "You would place close to Baz. And that Ryan's mostly talk — he came in twenty-fifth last year. With you we stand a good chance of winning."

"Well, it ain't gonna happen," said Matt.

"That's not fair," Gavin repeated for the third time.

"Fair or not, that's the way it is," said Matt.

They bounced the basketball a few more times. Then Gavin announced he had to go, and Robert looked at his watch and mumbled, and he left, too. Matt spent the next hour taking shots, pretending to care, pretending he was some place he had friends who really cared.

15

A Team Effort

On Wednesday, Matt returned to school. He dragged his feet along the asphalt path by the park, shuffled between the trees by the perimeter fence, and hoped no one would see him. He had just spent two days at home without TV.

The schoolyard before 9:00 buzzed with shrieks and laughter. Voices echoed off the corners of the brick building as kids ran, talked, bounced, hopped, jumped, and skidded in the early sunshine.

Matt had hoped to sneak up to the school undetected, to slip in the door as the bell rang. He would be happy if no one spoke to him all day. A small, bratty voice quickly dashed the possibility.

"Matt! Matt!" Gavin's voice pierced the ranks of children scattered across the playground.

Gavin grabbed Matt by the sleeve and tugged him toward a group of students huddled in the alcove next to the kindergarten. He could make out Robert, Kathryn, Baz, and Ashley. Many of the younger runners from the running group stood around, including Susan Singh and Bradley Fishback. He saw Ryan approaching from the other direction.

"Matt," said Robert, from near the middle of the group. "Welcome back. We missed you."

Kathryn smiled at him. "That really wasn't fair," she said. "That suspension, and you not being able to run on Friday."

Baz turned to him. "And we need you on the team. So, what we thought was, we'll go to see Mrs. MacMillan and ask her to let you run."

"What's that?" said Ryan, joining the group just in time to catch that last phrase. "No way. I don't care if this bozo runs."

"That's up to you, Ryan," said Baz. "But we think this whole thing is unfair to Matt."

"Besides," added Robert, "we do want to win the gold at Ganaraska, don't we?"

Ryan looked back at Robert. "You can do what you want," he said. "Just remember, if this guy runs, you don't, Maxwell."

Robert stared back. "I know that, Abolins."

"Be a loser if you want," Ryan said, turning away.

Robert watched him go, then gripped Gavin by one arm. "Looks as though we have one who votes no," he said. "But everybody else is in favour of asking the principal."

Leaving Matt behind, Robert led the group of runners to the front of the school. Gavin hurried along beside Robert. Ashley ruffled Gavin's hair, and smiled down on the younger boy.

In the main foyer they met a very surprised Ms. Wellesley.

"What's going on?" she asked, when the whole group shuffled to a halt in front of the principal's office.

"We're here to see Mrs. MacMillan," said Ashley.

"We think it is unfair that Matt can't run on Friday," added Robert. "So the whole cross-country team is using its right to protest."

Ms. Wellesley looked over the group with a slightly bemused look. "But Friday's meet has nothing to do with the whole running club."

Robert looked at her. "We have run with you all fall," he said.

"We've trained as a team. You have taught us to think like one."

"And," added Ashley, "as a team we think it is wrong that Matt can't run."

"But only the top three runners ... ," Ms. Wellesley began to reply before Kathryn interrupted her.

"No, no," she said. "The top three in each category run on Friday," she said. "But that's not the team. The team is everyone who has been running all fall. Every runner is part of the team."

"Well," said Ms. Wellesley, as though nothing more needed to be said.

"So we need to see Mrs. MacMillan," said Robert.

Ms. Wellesley peered around the group into the office. "I don't think she's available right now, but if you'll hang on a sec I'll check."

Mrs. MacMillan approached from the other end of the hallway.

"Well, well," she said. "Do we have a convention here?" Her voice, as always, was jovial, but the furrow in her brow showed how unusual she thought the gathering was.

"We represent, I mean we are, the cross-country team," said Robert. "We would like to talk to you about Matt. About his not being allowed to race on Friday."

Mrs. MacMillan glanced over the group — Robert, with Ashley, Kathryn, Hannah, Matt, Baz, Gavin, Bradley and more than a dozen others.

"Give me ten minutes, and we'll meet right after the announcements in the staff room."

A few of the younger students gasped at being allowed into that forbidden territory.

"Go to your classrooms for the opening exercises, and then I'll make an announcement to tell you when I've got the room cleared."

The principal left, and the runners milled about, their direction for the moment sapped.

"Think she'll say yes?" asked Ashley.

"I don't know," said Robert. "But at least she's going to hear what we have to say."

* * *

The S.T. Lovey Cross-Country Running Club — two dozen of them — squirmed on chairs in the staff room.

"This is where the teachers eat lunch," said Bradley. "Wow!"

Matt wasn't all that impressed, but said nothing.

But Mrs. MacMillan heard the comment as she entered. "I'm glad you are impressed," she said. "Now, what was it you wanted to talk about? Who is your spokesperson?"

Robert swiveled in his chair. "I guess that's Kathryn and I," he said.

The principal gestured to him. "What did you want to say?"

Robert cleared his throat, then looked down at his notes.

"We're members of the Running Club," Robert began. "And we don't think it's fair that Matt isn't allowed to race at Ganaraska."

Kathryn added, "We feel that he has finished his punishment now that his suspension is over."

"There's a lot here I can't discuss," Mrs. MacMillan said. "Matt's suspension was just part of it. There are other matters involved."

Robert said, "You mean, Matt not telling you that he was on the roof to rescue … somebody."

"Rescue?" said Mrs. MacMillan, surprised. "That's a pretty strong word. Can you explain?"

Kathryn said, "Gavin Richards has something to say."

Gavin stood up. "I was stuck on the roof that day," he said. "Matt got me down."

"Gavin, could you explain what you mean?" asked Mrs. MacMillan.

"High-school kids dared me," Gavin said. "I climbed up to see if I could do it."

"And you could."

"But when I got up there, I couldn't get down. And I tried to grab the pole with all the wires on it. And it leaned over something awful. Then the high-school kids said not to let go or the electricity would kill me. That's when—"

"When he started to cry," said Bradley. "That's when I ran to get Matt, because I knew he could get up there."

"And what did Matt do?" asked Mrs. MacMillan.

"He helped get Gavin down!" interjected Ashley, surprised. She finally connected what she had seen that day and the protest. "I saw him. He is a hero!"

"One at a time, Ashley," said Mrs. MacMillan. "Gavin has the floor."

"I was crying and I was scared," said Gavin. "Matt got me down, but then we saw you coming, and Bradley and I ran. And I know that was wrong, because Matt was just helping us. I mean me."

Mrs. MacMillan gave Gavin a piercing look. "Did Matt ask you to tell me this story?" she asked.

"No, Mrs. MacMillan. Matt didn't even know we were coming here today. But he's our friend, and I wouldn't want to see him punished for something that was my fault."

The room fell so silent they could hear the click-click of the clock on the wall.

At 9:30 exactly, the principal unpursed her lips and unfurrowed her brow.

"I thank you for this presentation," she said. "I will make a decision by noon tomorrow. Right now, I need to talk to Bradley and Gavin in my office. The rest of you can return to your classrooms."

Then, as an afterthought, she turned once more to face the group.

"I've been very impressed by your efforts here today," she said. "You obviously consider yourself a team. You have been mature and rational. Whatever my decision on Matt and Gavin, you should all be on hand to watch your teammates run. I will arrange for a bus to take all of the Running Club to Ganaraska Forest for the races on Friday."

"Does this mean we all get to run?" asked Hannah.

"No, I'm afraid those are rules I can't change," said Mrs. MacMillan. "But you can go as a team and you can cheer for your own teammates."

Ordinarily, such news would have sent them cheering. But until they knew the decision about Matt and Gavin, they couldn't celebrate.

On the way back to the classroom, Ashley walked beside Matt, twisting her blue hair band.

"I think you were great, rescuing Gavin," she said.

"Thanks."

"And I hope you can run on Friday. I really do. We're teammates, and I hope we can be friends."

16

Matt's News

By Friday morning, the day of the district cross-country championships at Ganaraska Forest, Matt had still not heard from the principal and had given up on any hope of running. He sat through math class, his mind drifting, trying to hide his disappointment. After the work that Robert and the others had done to get him reinstated, he wanted to see how well he could do; how well the team could do.

Matt turned around to see Ryan scowl and mouth something at him. He turned back to the front of the room. Ashley swivelled in her seat and flashed a smile.

Just then the classroom intercom crackled. "Ms. Wellesley, would you send Matt Thompson to the office please? Matt Thompson, to the office."

Everyone turned to look at him.

Matt stood, nervously adjusting his books.

Ms. Wellesley stood beside her desk, the way she had the first day. "Good luck, Matt," she said. "We're all hoping this works out."

The students nodded.

"Thanks," said Matt.

Ryan made a face and sneered. "I hope she fries your butt," he said in a whisper that everyone could hear.

Matt tried to ignore the comment as he slipped out the door into the deserted corridor and down the twenty-three steps to the principal's office.

Outside the office, Mr. Tuchuk was sweeping up the remains of a spilled kindergarten plant. He nodded knowingly.

Inside the office, a Grade One kid sniffled into his sleeve as he fidgeted on a too-tall chair.

The secretary looked up. "Oh, Matt. Mrs. MacMillan will see you now."

Mrs. MacMillan's fingers flew as she typed at the keyboard of a laptop computer. She didn't look around, but spoke quickly.

"Take a seat. I just want to finish this while I remember."

She finished typing with an exaggerated flourish and turned to Matt.

"I'll be brief," she said. "I know you are anxious about my decision. First, I think you should know that Gavin is being punished for his part in all this."

"Will he run be allowed to run today?" Matt asked.

"He'll tell you all about his detentions," said the principal. "But yes, he's still being allowed to run at Ganaraska. But now, I suppose you want to hear about my decision on you."

Matt nodded and listened as Mrs. MacMillan went on.

* * *

When Matt returned to the classroom, the whole class — all but Ryan — looked up. Twenty-nine pairs of eyes followed him to his desk, watched as he opened his binder.

"Well?" asked Ms. Wellesley, finally. It was five minutes before recess dismissal.

Matt bent down to search inside his desk for his math book. He looked up.

"Mrs. MacMillan said," he announced, "that …"

"Come on, come on," chanted his classmates.

"That my suspension …"

"Yes?" asked Ashley.

"… has been served and I'll be allowed to run today."

"That's great!" said Ashley. From the back of the room, Ryan groaned.

"Yea! Yea!" yelled several of his classmates.

"Congratulations," said Robert. He reached out to shake hands with Matt. "You deserve it." Only then did Matt realize that his reprieve meant Robert would not run.

He did not have time to mention it.

Ryan Abolins slammed his books shut and strode to the door.

"Who'd you get to fix things up for you, Thompson?" he snarled. He ripped at the door, as though he would pull it from its hinges. He flung back the door. "It's not fair!" he yelled. "Things were better last year before this clown came and ruined everything." He tried to slam the door as he headed out.

Matt rose from his desk.

"Class dismissed," said Ms. Wellesley.

Matt followed Ryan out the door. Ryan's reaction had surprised him. But then, Ryan had never really accepted the concept of a running team.

Mrs. MacMillan stood at her usual dismissal-time position in the school foyer.

Matt saw Ryan approach the glass doors to the foyer in full flight of anger. Without breaking stride, he raised his right foot to push it open. As he did, his left heel slipped on a wet spot on the floor. Matt watched as Ryan's foot smashed through the reinforced glass door.

The shattered glass slivers seemed to fall to the floor without sound. Ryan broke the silence with a long, loud scream of pain and fear that echoed up and down the corridors.

* * *

Ryan fell backward in slow motion. Matt realized that the glass shards that held Ryan's leg would grip like teeth as he fell. With one step he lunged forward, catching Ryan under the arms. Ms. Wellesley was at his side immediately, supporting Ryan's leg and slowly easing it out of the glass that held it.

"Easy now," said Mrs. MacMillan, as she came through the unbroken door. "Good work, Matt. Now let him down gently, that's it."

Mrs. MacMillan began re-routing students to other doors for the outdoor recess; Tony Tuchuk showed up almost instantly with a first aid kit. Robert was sent to the office to call 9-1-1 for an ambulance.

By the time the ambulance arrived, Ryan was resting on the floor, a pillow under his head, his leg elevated slightly and tightly bound with a tourniquet. Ambulance attendants surveyed the damage, checked Ryan's pulse, and rolled him onto a stretcher.

Ryan looked up at Mrs. MacMillan. "Now I know what you mean by inappropriate behaviour," he said, with a weak grin.

"You're a lucky boy," said the principal.

His rage now gone, Ryan winced. "I don't call this lucky," he said, pointing to his leg. "Now I won't be able to run this afternoon."

"No, that's true. It looks as though you've got a bad cut, and it'll take a few days to heal. But you could have done some pretty severe muscle damage."

"Is that right?" Ryan asked one of the paramedics. "Could I

have cut up the muscles in my leg?"

The attendant glanced at the shattered glass door.

"From the looks of that door, you could have severed tendons. If you'd done that, you'd never run again. I'd say you were pretty lucky someone caught you."

Mrs. MacMillan nodded. "It was Matt, here."

Ryan lifted his head as the attendants lifted the stretcher and began rolling it toward the waiting ambulance.

"Matt?" he said.

"Matt," said the principal.

As they rolled by, Matt reached out to grab Ryan's hand. Ryan pulled away, his frown turning back to a scowl.

He said nothing.

17

Ganaraska Rainbow

An hour and forty-five minutes later, a yellow school bus pulled up in front of S.T. Lovey Public School. A group of excited runners stood under the awning at the school entrance, out of the rain. The pure autumn sunshine of that morning had completely disappeared.

"I hope this rain stops," said Ashley. "It will ruin my hair and I'll look like a wet collie in the photographs."

"Oh, they'll cancel the races," said Baz. "You can't race when it's wet."

Robert looked at Baz and smiled. "This isn't a fair-weather sport like baseball," he said. "Cross-country running takes place in rain, snow, and freezing weather."

"How would you know that, Robert?" asked Matt.

"He reads the encyclopedia," said Baz with a laugh.

Robert smiled back. "I read it last night in a sports magazine. It's true. Lightning wouldn't be good, but a little rain will just make it uncomfortable for people to watch."

"Sounds like fun!" said Gavin.

"What about Ryan?" Kathryn asked. "Is he going to be able to run?"

Ms. Wellesley had been talking to the bus driver. Now she stepped off the bus and walked to the group at the school entrance.

She lifted a hand to get everyone's attention. "Ryan's going to be okay," she said. "But he has a bad gash in his leg. It's not that serious, but he won't be able to run today."

"Does that mean Robert is going to run?" asked Kathryn.

"That's a detail to look after when we get there. However, does everybody like rain?" she asked.

"We'll beat 'em in any weather," said Baz.

"But my hair!" cried Ashley. "And the mud! The whole course will be covered with mud, and it'll be slippy and messy and yuck!"

"Ashley," said Ms. Wellesley, "you'll do much better if you think less about your hair and your boyfriends and more about the race. You're going to get wet and muddy, so get used to it."

Ashley looked up at Ms. Wellesley. She twirled a piece of hair in her left hand. She thought for a minute, and then asked permission to leave the bus.

Mr. Tuchuk came around the corner of the building and stood by bus.

"How did you make out last weekend, Fran?" he asked Ms. Wellesley.

Matt watched as his teacher turned to the custodian with a smile. "At High Park? It was a good day."

"I had to leave before your race started," Mr. Tuchuk said. "How'd it go?"

Ms. Wellesley beamed. "Great race," she said. "I came first."

Tony turned to Matt. "Hear that? Your coach took first place in the Toronto Road Runners Cross-Country Championship. That's the kind of coaching you've had this year."

Matt said, "You mean, really?"

Tony laughed. "You didn't know? Your coach, Fran Wellesley, beat some of the best runners in the country. She's a champion."

Ashley came out of the school carrying her backpack and returned to the bus. "Champion?" she said. "Wow!"

She clutched her pencil box in her left hand.

At 12:30 exactly, the bus pulled slowly away from the school. On board were twenty-two students, Ms. Wellesley, the Phys. Ed. teacher, two parent volunteers, and Mrs. Gibner, a jaunty-looking school bus driver who thought she had seen everything.

The route to Ganaraska Forest took them along Highway 2 through downtown Bowmanville, past neat dairy farms and manicured subdivisions, past the Bowmanville Zoo.

The bus turned north on Highway 115, finally exiting on a secondary road. The windshield wipers continued working as a sudden shower of rain pelted on the metal roof of the bus. Behind them, the sun broke through the clouds.

Gavin was the first to see the rainbow.

It was a full half-circle of rich colours across the sky. "Look everybody!" Gavin said, pointing. "A rainbow! And the pot of gold is right there at Ganaraska!"

The passengers jostled for a better view, craning their necks and looking up to see the whole colourful spectacle.

"Ganaraska Gold!" yelled Baz. "That's what we're after today! Gold!"

"Gold, gold, gold," yelled the students in a rhythmic chant.

After two more turns along a narrow country road, the bus groaned its way under the dripping wet leaves of maple trees and lurched to a stop in an overcrowded parking lot.

Ms. Wellesley stood by the driver while the students wriggled in their seats. Slowly, the bus grew quiet. "Three things. First, our parent volunteers today are Mr. Hopley and Mrs. MacLean. They're here to help."

The students applauded.

"They're going to get off first and set up our tarpaulin and flag, so everybody knows where our home base is.

"Second, you must be gathered by our home base at 2:45.

"Third, because you people have pulled together as a team so well, I have something special for you." She reached into a plastic bag.

"I have here the S.T. Lovey Cross-Country Team T-shirt. There's one for each of you!"

"All right! All right!" The shouts rang around the bus.

"She means the guys who are racing today, not you !" said Ashley.

"No," said Ms. Wellesley, "not just the runners. There is one for everyone. You are the team from Lovey. I expect everyone to wear this shirt today. That includes parents and coaches. We're all part of the same team, and we'll all know who we are."

More shouts and cheers.

"Can I keep it?" asked Gavin. "Is it mine?"

"You wear this shirt today, and you can keep it forever. It's yours."

The bus rocked with the cheers.

The students filed off the bus, slowly, into the fine mist. The sun peeked out. Each person who stepped off the bus was handed an emerald green T-shirt. After the first few had struggled into the shirt, you could see the crest across the front: *S.T. Lovey Cross-Country*.

Slashing across the front was a rainbow, thick at one end and arcing to the right.

"The rainbow is a coincidence," Ms. Wellesley said, as they milled around admiring their new team uniform. "And maybe next year we can think of a better team name."

Ashley held her T-shirt in front of her to estimate the fit. "How's this look?" she asked Matt.

Matt stumbled and grasped his T-shirt, and looked at Ashley as though he had not seen her. "It's … it's great," he said.

18

Ashley's Surprise

Matt and his teammates lined up to watch the running of the junior races. Because of the rain, the junior boys and girls raced together.

"That's going to make it tough at the start," said Ms. Wellesley. "It's going to be crowded — worse than usual."

The first 100 metres of the course swept across a wide stretch of open park. Then it narrowed into an uphill trail, lined by red-leaved sumac.

Matt stood with his team and watched as more than 100 junior runners tensed, waiting for the starter's signal. Gavin, short even among his own age group, toed the line. The starter blew the whistle and lowered his arm. The first race was on.

Gavin sprinted across the park in the first wave of runners. By time he reached the foot of the hill where the course narrowed, he was in tenth place. Not bad, Matt thought, and well ahead of the jostling mob behind.

The team watched as the runners worked for position. Once they started up the hill on the narrow trail, there would be little room for passing until almost half-way through the race. Some runners at the back of the pack had started walking while still in the park.

"Looks as though they could have used some training," said

Ashley. "I'm sure glad we had it."

But within three minutes, the last runner had disappeared up the hill. The team shifted, lining up along the ropes marking the finishing chute.

"The juniors run 1 kilometre," said Ms. Wellesley. "The winners should take about four minutes or so."

At the finish, the runners had to scurry down a steep slope, emerging onto the final 100 metres of open park that sloped gently down to the finish-chute.

Yells and grunts reached the finishers as they came down that last slope. First to burst from under the canopy of trees was Gavin. Behind him by 2 metres ran a dark-haired girl.

"Come on, Lovey, come on Lovey," shouted Gavin's teammates.

At the bottom of the hill, Gavin lost his cap to a sumac branch. He was up on his toes then, sprinting, his face drawn tight, his determination showing.

Half-way to the finish-line, the girl pulled even with Gavin. Gavin glanced sideways, then surged to prevent her from passing. The two sprinted, flat-out, side by side to the finish line.

"Way to go, Lovey, way to go Lovey," shouted the team.

Ten minutes later, when all the junior runners had completed the course and places were recorded, the senior girls began to line up.

"Senior girls, Grades Seven and Eight," said the announcer into a microphone. "Senior girls, please line up."

When the runners were all in place, spread out seventy-five wide along a thin line, the starter held up her arm. For a frozen moment nothing moved. Then the starter's arm came down, and the shrill whistle pierced the autumn air.

The runners were off.

"Senior girls, one-and-a-half kilometres," said Ms. Wellesley.

"Maybe seven to eight minutes."

They watched as Kathryn pulled ahead, first to start up the hill where the trail narrowed, first to be swallowed by the sumacs. Ashley followed in tenth place. Further back, almost hidden in a mob of runners, was Hannah, her long ponytail bouncing under her baseball cap.

When the runners had all cleared the open part of the park, the team resumed their watch by the finish-chute. They had barely elbowed their way into position when the sky opened up.

The rain came down in torrents. By the time people realized they could get soaked, they were. Many ran for shelter under the tarpaulin where the race officials stood; others headed for whatever shelter they could find.

But soaked is soaked.

The S.T. Lovey team held their position on both sides of the finish-chute, waiting for the leaders to appear.

First was Kathryn, chased down the final stretch by one other girl, equally drenched. But Kathryn's final surge ended any hopes her opponent might have had.

Two, three more runners appeared. Then came Ashley, and the Lovey team erupted in cheers.

Like other runners, Ashley was soaked. She was also mud-splattered from a fall. Her knees, her thighs, the front of her new emerald green T-shirt, even her face and hair were caked in one smear of greasy brown mud.

But what the Lovey team saw was not the mud, but the fire in her eyes as she spotted the finish-line. Other runners appeared to wilt and relax once in sight of the finish-line. Not Ashley. She rose on her toes into a fierce sprint that took her past one, two, then three runners.

Third Place. The Lovey cheer drowned out the rain.

A few minutes later, Ashley returned to the team's home base, caked in mud, her clothes soaked, her eyes dancing as though she had never been more proud.

"Great race," Matt said.

"Thanks," Ashley replied. "I fell at the top of that last hill, just *zip*, *splat*! And I skidded face-first down the hill. I thought I was done. Then I said, what the heck, I can't get any muddier or any wetter."

"That's the spirit," said Ms. Wellesley.

"Thanks. How are we doing?"

"Well, thanks to you, we're in second, after Dobbs."

"How do they figure that out?"

"They add up the finishing places," Ms. Wellesley said. "The school team with the lowest total from all the races wins the gold medal. It's that simple."

"We've got three first. We should be leading," said Kathryn.

"Junior girls we placed second, seventh and eleventh; in the boys, first, eleventh and twenty-third. That's, hmm, fifty-five points. Senior girls were first, third, and twentieth. That's, let's see, seventy-nine points. It puts us in second place, only a half-dozen points out of first."

"You mean with firsts in every race, we're still behind Dobbs?" asked Ashley.

"The third runner on each team counts just as much," said Ms. Wellesley, "maybe more. Our first runner will beat Dobbs' runners by two, three places. But their third runners are beating us by seven or eight places."

"Wow! This means everything counts," said Robert.

"Every runner you pass counts as a point for our team." Ms. Wellesley paused, then turned to Robert.

"Robert, I have to make sure you're signed up."

Robert looked up. "Rob," he replied. "Please have them call me Rob."

"Rob it is. We're in a great position now," said Ms. Wellesley. "Now it's all up to you senior boys. Give it everything you've got."

Matt could see the look in Rob's eyes. He had wished for this chance, had trained for this chance.

Baz came over. He placed one arm on Matt's shoulder, one on Rob's. "This is it, guys. It's all up to us. Just remember: every single runner we pass is a point for the team. We're team-mates. Let's do it!"

19

Ganaraska Gold

Matt Thompson tensed at the starting line, legs trembling, but not from the cold or the steady rain. Runners beside and behind him jostled for position, but he resisted. On the sidelines, where his team had gathered, he could see Ashley smiling at him, then leaning over to place Gavin's cap back on his head.

He remembered the first day he had met Gavin, and his adventure on the portable roof. His thoughts flicked to the rescue, and to his suspension, and how his new friends had come to his aid.

And now he had to do his best.

"Ready!" shouted the starter, arm raised.

Runners leaned forward, arms cocked like pistons.

The starter's arm came down, and the whistle sounded.

The field of runners sprinted forward, slipping and splashing, as though in a 100-metre dash. Matt pressed hard, determined not to be buried in the pack. For a moment Matt could see Rob, taller than almost everyone. To his left, Baz's wet black hair glistened. Then Matt felt himself bumped and jostled.

When the first runner entered the wooded trail, Matt was 20 metres and twenty runners back. Baz had pulled into third place. On the sidelines, the Lovey team yelled and screamed encouragement.

"Go, Lovey, go! Go, Lovey, go!"

And when they saw him, "Matt-ee! Matt-ee!"

Up the narrow trail, he focused on the runner ahead. Shoes slithered on the slippery mud. His legs felt waterlogged, quivering with fatigue. The runner ahead of him stopped to walk. Matt stepped by him, slipped, and caught his balance with two hands in the mud. *Every runner I pass counts*, he reminded himself.

At the top, the trail widened. Strangely, now that the woods allowed room to pass, the runners strung out single file, settling into a race rhythm. Rain ran off Matt's hair into his eyes. He wiped his brow with one motion, moved up behind one runner, then two, pushing strongly to go by. Three, four.

Breath came in deep draughts now; his legs churned. Each time he passed another runner he pushed beyond his fatigue, surprised each time to find his body, his legs responding. Two, three more runners. Mud flung into the air from churning feet. Four, five, six. Each counted.

Up ahead the leader, followed by Baz, turned sharply to the right out of sight. One, two. He counted as others followed: three, four, five, six.

Matt passed another runner as he turned the corner himself, another on the downgrade. Fifth place. Then he slithered on his hands and knees up a steep slope, soupy with mud, catching two more by midway.

Third.

He came over the top. Only two runners remained ahead: Baz and the leader, a brown-haired boy from Dodds. They were only metres ahead as they began the treacherous, muddy descent down the final hill.

Danger, *danger*, *danger*, Matt told himself as he careered down that final slope. He propelled himself with gravity, deftly avoiding slippery pockets of mud and water, his feet flying from knoll to turf-covered knoll, his arms like wings to balance his flight down the hill.

Ahead, Baz darted to the right. At the same time, the leader hit a hollow with his right heel and skidded, tripping Baz. The pair went down in one heap, skidding down the brisk slope, Baz face-first in the mud.

Matt, eight strides behind, saw them spin and fall. He checked his pace and leaped over the fallen runners.

First place!

He hung in the air as the ground dropped away under him, landing on a strip muddy as a hog's bath. For a moment he was fine, surfing down the depression, until both feet went out from under him. He landed flat-out, face-first in a puddle of mud.

Baz and the opponent from Dodds continued their downhill skid, stopped only when one of them — Matt never did find out which — pushed Matt's face down for one last taste of soupy grime.

All three were up together as though they had not missed a step. Baz was still in second, with Matt again third, still five steps behind. The mud made chocolate soldiers of each — shoes, socks, shorts, shirt, face, and hair, all plastered with a mud coat.

Matt emerged into the park clearing, now just off Baz's shoulder and 5 metres behind the leader.

In the distance, where the orange traffic cones narrowed to the finish, Matt could see his family: his father, mouth open and fists pumping; his mother, crying; between them, Cathy-Marie, shouting like a foghorn. Nearby, still dressed in his green coveralls, hardly hidden with a makeshift raincoat, Tony Tuchuk pumped both of his sinewy arms and shouted through his mustache. Mrs. MacMillan, in a shiny, hooded red raincoat and matching red boots, guarded the finish-line like a grown-up Red Riding Hood.

And Ryan. On crutches. In the rain.

Yelling.

All soundless, as Matt's senses turned inward, to the race,

to the runner beside him, to his fatigue.

Surges, Ms. Wellesley? A hundred left feet?

He rose on his toes, his arms pumping, his knees lifting —
a sprint, that finishing kick when legs hurt and lungs burn and
time stands still. The crowd roared and jumped and shouted, but
Matt heard only the wall of sound and saw only the narrowing
line of cones and the finish tape and the mud and the rain and
Baz's mud-caked shoulders as he passed. Matt was even with
the leader now, shoulder to shoulder, stride for stride.

Take my lumps, Mom and Dad?

The crowd screamed, the Lovey squad in their team shirts
loudest of all, the roar filling his ears, his lungs, his heart. His
cramped legs powered on their own, his heavy arms moved in
their own rhythm. His lungs burned with each gasp of welcome
air, his parched mouth dribbling spittle on his chin. He floated,
airborne, between strides.

Pump! Lift!

The leader faltered for only for a half-step, but Matt knew
the chance was his. He knew the surge was working, sensed the
leader's hesitation, happy for second place.

Matt was a metre clear, one step, two steps — and he hit
the tape.

First place!

Arms reached out to pat his back as he bent over in the chute.
He straightened and turned in time to see Baz kick home, not
quite able to catch the Dodds runner, a half-pace back in third.

His parents reached him in the finish-chute, and hugged
him, soaked and muddy.

"Way to go, son. We're so proud."

"Dad. You got here. I didn't think—"

"I took the rest of the day off. My teammates at work
pushed me out the door. And Cathy-Marie had planned since

yesterday to surprise you. If you ran."

"Great run, brother," said Cathy-Marie.

Mr. Thompson grasped his son's hand, an overhand shake. "Great job!"

Matt checked in at the officials' table, then turned back to his parents.

"We've got one more teammate out on the course," he said. "We've got to wait for Rob Maxwell."

Matt moved around the side of the finish-chute and edged along to find a place well in sight of the finishing runners. He felt someone grab his elbow.

"Up here," said Baz, guiding him further away from the finish-line. "He won't be able to see us in the crowd. If we move up here, he'll see us as soon as he comes around that last bend at the bottom of the hill."

Matt nodded, saw that Baz was right. Ashley ran up to them.

"Let's cheer Rob in," she said.

They found a position at the edge of the roped-off area, about 20 metres from the last bend. Just in time. Several runners by now had passed — ten, maybe a dozen.

Now Rob stumbled down the hill, almost off balance. Baz and Matt and Ashley and the rest of the team who had joined them jumped and yelled: "Go, Rob, go! Go, Rob, go!"

Rob caught his balance in one step. They could see him rise on his toes, his stride now landing mid-foot, as he kicked and passed one, two, three more runners before he disappeared into the mob beyond the finish-line.

"Six! He caught six more!" said Baz.

"I counted seven!" said Ashley.

"Let's hear it for Lovey! Let's hear it for Lovey!"

And then they rejoined their teammates to wait for the final tally.

The Winner is …

Returning to S.T. Lovey Public School, Ms. Wellesley ordered the school bus to pull into the parking lot of a pizza parlour in Bowmanville.

"What about the bus?" someone asked. "I thought we had to go back."

"Mrs. MacMillan arranged this," said Ms. Wellesley, "so we could celebrate!"

The busload erupted in a cheer.

It was a muddy group that placed orders and spread themselves over several tables in the pizza shop. Ms. Wellesley walked among them, offering congratulations.

"I can't believe we won the championship," said Rob, when she stopped at his table."

"Ahead of Dobbs," said Baz. "By one point!"

"The guy that Matt passed!" added Kathryn.

"Everyone that Kathryn passed," said Gavin.

"Everyone that I passed!" said Ashley.

"The six guys Rob passed at the finish!" said Matt. "Rob won the day."

Ms. Wellesley nodded and smiled.

"Dobbs tied for second," she said. "One point behind. Every single runner each of you passed gave us the championship.

This is a team win, and not just a win for those who ran today — they represented this team."

"Right," said Gavin. "Everybody passed somebody."

"And cheered!" added Kathryn. "That sure helped a lot when it was needed."

Ashley looked at Ms. Wellesley.

"I didn't agree when you started talking about teamwork," she said. "I thought it was enough just to go out and run my fastest. Those surges and stuff helped make all the runners faster. And having the team to cheer sure helped."

"You've become a good team player, Ashley," Ms. Wellesley said. "Now, it's a long time until spring. How many here are interested in training for track and field for next year?"

Hands shot up.

"Is it muddy?" asked Ashley, and everyone laughed.

"Me, too," said Ryan. "If my leg is okay by then."

"And how many are interested in training this winter?"

The hands went up again.

"Training in the winter?" asked Gavin. "You can't run in snow."

"You didn't melt in the rain today," said Ms. Wellesley. "In fact, you all look as though you could use some hosing down. A little snow just makes the ground softer. You can also run on an indoor track at the Ottawa Civic Dome."

The team cheered as Ms. Wellesley raised the trophy over her head.

Ashley sat at a table, her green team shirt brown with mud, hunched over her pencil box. Carefully, she had covered the case with whiteout, and was now painting a new name on the box.

"Who is it this time, Ash?" asked Baz. "Are there any boys left?"

Ashley looked up, made a face at Baz, and then smiled at Matt, her eyes resting on him just long enough to make him blush.

She held up the pencil box.

In neat letters it read: *ASHLEY GROVIER, S.T. LOVEY X-COUNTRY*.

The pizza parlour manager walked over.

"Cross-country runners, eh?" he said. "Who's the champion?"

Baz pointed to Kathryn and to Matt. "These two both placed first."

Gavin stood on a chair to be noticed.

"We're the S.T. Lovey Cross-Country Team," he replied. "We won the team championship. We're all champions."

Other books you'll enjoy in the Sports Stories series...

Running

❏ *Fast Finish* by Bill Swan #30
Noah is a promising young runner headed for the provincial finals when he suddenly decides to withdraw from the event.

❏ *Mud Run* by Bill Swan #60
No one in the S.T. Lovey Cross-Country Club is running with the pack, until the new coach demonstrates the value of teamwork.

Track and Field

❏ *Mikayla's Victory* by Cynthia Bates #29
Mikayla must compete against her friend if she wants to represent her school at an important track event.

❏ *Walker's Runners* by Robert Rayner #55
Toby Morton hates gym. In fact, he doesn't run for anything — except the classroom door. Then Mr. Walker arrives and persuades Toby to join the running team.

Baseball

❏ *Curve Ball* by John Danakas #1
Tom Poulos is looking forward to a summer of baseball in Toronto until his mother puts him on a plane to Winnipeg.

❏ *Baseball Crazy* by Martyn Godfrey #10
Rob Carter wins an all-expenses-paid chance to be bat boy at the Blue Jays spring training camp in Florida.

❏ *Shark Attack* by Judi Peers #25
The East City Sharks have a good chance of winning the county championship until their arch rivals get a tough new pitcher.

❏ *Hit and Run* by Dawn Hunter and Karen Hunter #35
Glen Thomson is a talented pitcher, but as his ego inflates, team morale plummets. Will he learn from being benched for losing his temper?

❏ *Power Hitter* by C. A. Forsyth #41
Connor's summer was looking like a write-off. That is, until he discovered his secret talent.

❏ *Sayonara, Sharks* by Judi Peers #48
In this sequel to *Shark Attack*, Ben and Kate are excited about the school trip to Japan, but Matt's not sure he wants to go.

Soccer

❏ *Lizzie's Soccer Showdown* by John Danakas #3
When Lizzie asks why the boys and girls can't play together, she finds herself the new captain of the soccer team.

❏ *Alecia's Challenge* by Sandra Diersch #32
Thirteen-year-old Alecia has to cope with a new school, a new step-father, and friends who have suddenly discovered the opposite sex.

❏ *Shut-Out!* by Camilla Reghelini Rivers #39
David wants to play soccer more than anything, but will the new coach let him?

❏ *Offside!* by Sandra Diersch #43
Alecia has to confront a new girl who drives her teammates crazy.

❏ *Heads Up!* by Dawn Hunter and Karen Hunter #45
Do the Warriors really need a new, hot-shot player who skips practice?

❏ *Off the Wall* by Camilla Reghelini Rivers #52
Lizzie loves indoor soccer, and she's thrilled when her little sister gets into the sport. But when their teams are pitted against each other, Lizzie can only warn her sister to watch out.

❏ *Trapped!* by Michele Martin Bossley #53
There's a thief on Jane's soccer team, and everyone thinks it's her best friend, Ashley. Jane must find the true culprit to save both Ashley and the team's morale.

❏ *Soccer Star!* by Jacqueline Guest #61
Samantha longs to show up Carly, the school's reigning soccer star, but her new interest in theatre is taking up a lot of her time. Can she really do it all?